AN OZARKS CHRISTMAS

ANGELA DRAKE

AN OZARKS CHRISTMAS is book one of the Planned to Perfection series.

Cover – Sweet 'N Spicy Designs

Creative Dreams Press.
Birch Tree, MO

ISBN: 978-1-7328053-0-9

DEDICATION

To my husband. Without him none of my dreams
would be possible.

.

ACKNOWLEDGMENTS

To the people of Eureka Springs who always make me feel at home. A big thank you to my sprint partners, June, Kathy, Pam and Tara who provide the swift kick of encouragement when necessary. Last but not least, to Sharon Holmes for her amazing patience. Each of you played an important part in making this book possible. Thank you from the bottom of my heart.

CHAPTER 1

Stephanie sat in one of the chairs on the patio of the Crescent Hotel, letting the peace of the valley beyond wash over her. She needed the calming effect the Ozarks community offered. A star fell from the velvet sky. She closed her eyes.

"I wish I may, I wish I might have the wish I wish tonight."

She struggled between wishing Brendan wasn't in the ballroom behind her and thankful for his agreeing to lend his talents to the Santa Club Gala. If she could just avoid seeing him for another hour, she could go back to her cottage down the road without having to come face to face with her past. "I wish…"

"May I join you?"

So much for wishes. Her heart felt as if a beat had skipped then fluttered back to life. She knew without looking the voice belonged to Brendan Keane – entertainer, playboy, and thief. Focusing on her wish, she hadn't heard him open nor close the ballroom door as he came outside.

Glancing to her left she could see the tall, strong frame of the man she couldn't forget. The man who had stolen her heart so long ago.

"Of course." She struggled to keep her voice even. She wanted to tell him to go away. Not just from the hotel but from the close-knit community she called home. She hadn't wanted him here from the beginning but her ultimate goal for the event to be a success over-ruled. This fundraiser would ensure that every child in Eureka Springs and the surrounding area would receive a visit from Santa Claus. Being the biggest draw in the music business, Brendan Keane would make that possible. The fact he had volunteered to perform was a big boost to the benefit's bottom line.

"I'm sorry if I intruded."

An apology? In all their time together she'd never heard him apologize for anything – and he'd had plenty of occasions.

"Not at all. I need to go back in anyway." She hated that her voice shook. His mere presence shouldn't be affecting her.

The scent of his cologne drifted on the air. Her skin tingled from the nearness of him as memories of his touch raced through her mind. A feeling of comfort mixed with something else she didn't want to acknowledge needled at her heart.

Brendan sat down a couple of chairs over from her, lacing his fingers across his midsection and stretching his legs out in front of him. Stephanie watched his languid movement. She had seen him relaxed many times in their time together. Then he had needed alcohol to produce the effect. She braced the palms of her hands on the chair arms, preparing to rise.

"It's a beautiful evening." His deep vibrato halted her escape. The same tone that had seduced her a lifetime ago. After thirteen years his voice still mesmerized her, pouring over her in a sweet caress. Some memories seemed to overshadow the ones of the drunk she had finally seen him for.

Through connections with his family she had never seen a reason to dissolve she knew he was approaching his thirteenth year of sobriety. She didn't know what had finally triggered him turning his life around but like everything else Brendan did, he gave it his all. His success was a shining example.

She had wanted permanence and a family, the two things his addiction had prevented them from sharing when she had been sure they belonged together. Now Brendan's career had become a different form of addiction.

Though she had walked away from Brendan, she stayed close with his family. Something she knew he was still trying to rebuild. They were all a part of what he'd felt unimportant at the time.

For Stephanie, his parents were the ones she never had. Her mother had died of heart failure when Stephanie was twelve, the point in her life when she had needed her mom the most. Dad and Brendan shared the same ailment, but unlike the love of her life, Dad got mean. There were a lot of times she found safety in Brendan's little house across the river. His sister, Kris, served as maid of honor in her wedding to Matthew and his dad walked her down the aisle. Thankfully, they hadn't made a trip to Eureka Springs since she and the kids moved down here.

The only part of her past her friend, Jennifer, knew about was her tragic loss of Matthew and the two beautiful children they'd had. Most of the time she tried to pretend Brendan had never been a part of her life, a task that became more and more difficult when she looked at her daughter, Kim. The older she became, the more she resembled him. Not the man she grew up calling Dad.

"There are several businesses on the program. Is one of them yours?"

"I helped plan the event. I own Planned to Perfection.

She'd managed to avoid introductions until now. The avoidance had required a trip out of town with the children so she didn't run into him until she absolutely had to, arriving back with just enough time to dress and arrive fashionably late.

"Then you know the hotel manager. Jennifer's my daughter."

Jennifer didn't remember Stephanie as a part of her childhood or her dad's life and Stephanie wasn't ready to reveal that part of her to the young woman who had become an incredible friend. Stephanie knew this day would come. She was planning Jennifer's wedding, after all. Until he had volunteered his services for tonight she had thought she had a good four months to prepare for the moment when she'd have to face him. Yet, here he was.

The pride in his voice shone like the ballroom chandelier. Where had that pride been when Jennifer was a child? When the little girl should be looking up to her father as the greatest man to walk the earth, she was looking out a window wondering if he'd even remember her birthday, school program or Christmas?

"Yes, I do. Speaking of, I must get back to the guests." As she stood and turned towards the doors, she realized too late that she had emerged from the shadow, the lights from above shining like a spotlight.

"Stephanie?"

She froze, mid-step as if avoiding quicksand. He was capable of weaving a spell she didn't want to fall under. When she had walked away from him that late summer day a lifetime ago, she swore he would never have emotional control over her again. With Matthew she had become her own person. A person fate had been preparing her for. She didn't need his shoulder to cry on, or his body to protect her. She wouldn't fall back to being less than what she had become.

"Stephanie."

She felt more than heard the reverence as he repeated her name. The tone enveloping them in a cloud of memories. She pulled her shawl tighter around her shoulders, struggling to suppress the flood of emotions she'd anticipated for weeks. Feelings long-buried engulfed her to the core. She had survived them all over the years to be drenched in them here, now.

"Hello, Brendan." Her business tone belied the

turbulent battle waging within her.

He stood, rallying to his full 6'3" and moved to embrace her. She took a step back. If she'd learned anything from her past, his touch would be her undoing. From the moment she knew Brendan was coming she'd made a firm promise to herself that Brendan Keane would not touch her in any way shape or form. There was a time when she willingly allowed herself the safety of his arms. She didn't need him or any support he thought to offer. She didn't need him in her life at all.

He tucked his hands into the front pockets of his black trousers. He'd always been a snappy dresser. That and his charming ways had earned him the nickname, Playboy. He was right out of a 1970's romance. Though he'd been an alcoholic, he'd seldom appeared drunk. Even the clothes he wore on the construction site looked fresh out of his closet when he'd come into the bar after work where she waitressed. Then and now he looked irresistible.

"Brendan, when I agreed to your offer, I had no intention of seeing you other than from the back of the ballroom. At least, not before Jennifer's wedding in December."

"Seriously? I've spent the past twelve years figuring out what I'd say when I saw you again."

She listened, waiting for words that wouldn't change anything. She wanted to believe the steps in the program had led him to some personal discoveries, realizations of what a jerk he had been and how he had hurt those who loved him... herself included.

"I can't believe you're here."

"My family moved down here a couple of years ago."

Never in her entire life had she felt so much a part of a community as she did here in Eureka Springs. This was the perfect place to raise a family. The over-all ambiance of the quaint Victorian tourist town soothed the spirit. But tonight she didn't think anything could bring her peace of mind.

"You have children?"

Something deep inside compelled her to answer his question rather than run for her life.

"Yes. Kimberley is twelve and Max is two." She smiled, remembering how the Santa Club had come to be and the reason for his presence. "Kim was in fourth grade when she came home one afternoon just devastated. The first graders wrote paragraphs about 'Why I Believe in Santa'. The teacher hung them along the hall for everyone to enjoy. Kim read enough to realize that a large number of the kids didn't believe in Santa because he never came to their house."

"Everyone should believe in Santa Claus at some point in their life."

"She thought so, too. She was at the age where she understood about the 'Spirit of the Season'. She wanted to clean out her and Max's toys and give away everything they owned.

"She sounds like a compassionate young lady?"

"Kimmie is my dynamo promoter. She convinces everyone it's their duty to contribute in some way."

This was a special night at the Crescent Hotel.

Known world-wide as the Grand Old Lady of the Ozarks, the hotel sat on a hill overlooking Eureka Springs Arkansas. Tonight, in spite of the late summer heat, everyone in the business community was dancing and laughing while giving money to their favorite charity.

Kimberly's generous spirit had prompted Stephanie and some of her new friends in town to form the club that first year. She wanted to help restore faith in Santa in the hearts of children and grownups alike.

"Thank you for doing this."

"When Jennifer told me the event was coming up, I knew I wanted to help out. Kids have always been important to me."

"Since when?" She had no control over the fire and ice accompanying her words.

"What's that supposed to mean?"

"As I recall, kids were not a priority for you when Jennifer was growing up. So important you couldn't sober up long enough to take responsibility for her. Why should you care about someone else's children?"

"That's not fair Steph, and you know it. I'd have done anything for Jennifer. She is my daughter, for God's sakes! Debbie wouldn't let me anywhere near her."

"Anything but stop drinking. Debbie didn't want her little girl to know she had a drunk for a father." Every fiber of her being shook with pent up anger at what his problem had cost so many people. "And I'd been naïve enough to think you'd stop for me."

She turned to go into the lobby as Brendan

grabbed her arm, forcing her to face him.

"Let me go!"

"Will you hear me out?"

"Why should I? She felt the tears run like a flooded river down her cheeks. She was conscious of the music growing louder then recede and turned her head to see Jennifer closing the door as she joined them on the patio.

"What is going on out here?"

"Just a small miscommunication, sweetheart." His vision never wavered from hers. His eyes reminded her of chocolate drops, now hardened as if seized.

"They are almost through announcing the silent auction winners. You're up next."

"I think you should do what you came for." Frost could have formed on her words but Stephanie didn't care. This evening was turning out just as she knew it would.

"Wouldn't want to keep my public waiting, would we?" His steel voice stabbed her heart, hitting the mark as he brushed past the two women and into the hotel lobby.

"Are you okay, Steph?"

Okay? Not even close. She knew how tonight would go and no amount of wishing on a star would change the outcome. Brendan still seemed to see at least parts of his past through rose colored glasses. Stephanie had taken her own off the day she had walked away, crushing the imaginary lenses with every step.

Looking at Brendan's daughter she saw the resemblance she had noted during their first meeting. Through Brendan's parents, she had kept track of Jennifer and while she hadn't wanted to divulge her past, she did make sure to introduce herself to the Crescent Hotel manager as soon as a business opportunity arose. She knew now that after tonight's confrontation with him, it would only be a matter of time before her secret came out.

"I'll be fine. Nothing a little sleep won't cure." She rubbed trembling fingers across her temples in an attempt to ease some of the throbbing. "I'm just beat."

"You've been working too hard putting this shindig together. I can close things down here if you want to go snuggle with the kids."

"I think I'll do that. Kimberly is home with Max. I promised her I'd be home to tuck them in." Floodgates of the pent-up nerves opened and she quickly swiped at tears forming before they could begin to overflow. She pulled Jennifer in for a hug. "We'll talk tomorrow and you can give me the rundown."

"Alright. I'll come by in the morning for coffee. The baker will have fresh croissants. I'll bring some."

"Sounds wonderful. Goodnight."

After Jennifer went back inside, Stephanie turned back to the view from the patio. Taking a cleansing breath, she allowed the peacefulness of the Ozarks to overtake her senses.

She closed her eyes, remembering the first time she had heard him sing. He often played drums along with the stereo when she visited. His house was her haven and she knew he would always keep her safe. She spent a lot of time curled up on the couch watching the man behind the drums, giving in to the beat and pretending for the moment there was no other place or people in the world – just Brendan, herself and the night.

Their time together often included sex. She didn't know much about protection and she never thought about needing any when they were together. Being with Brendan was all that mattered. She had been eight years his junior, only eighteen, but none of that seemed important.

Feeling loved in the only way she knew he was capable of expressing the emotion was what mattered. On one of their last nights together he had asked why she kept coming back. Naively she had answered that they were good together. She soon realized there were more important things in life.

Applause brought her back to the present. She had a new safe haven now and that's just where she needed to be. Adjusting her shawl, she stepped off the patio and went through the garden to the parking lot. She couldn't face anyone else tonight. The thank-you cards she would mail tomorrow would have to suffice.

Letting herself in the house on Pine Street, Stephanie checked on the children before going down the hall to her own room. Within moments of crawling under the covers and closing her eyes vision of a tall dark-haired man with warm brown eyes appeared. She groaned as she rolled onto her side, pulling the pillow over her head. But the pillow couldn't keep her thoughts from running rampant. The truth was that after all these years, the sight of Brendan Keane still affected her like no other man she had ever known, including her beloved Matthew. But it was too late for them. Childhood fantasies of Santa Claus and wishes were one thing, but in the adult world there was no going back.

* * *

Making his set as short as possible, he'd gone in search of Stephanie. He stood outside of the hotel, scanning the empty darkness as he raked a hand through his hair in frustration. Of all the places to run into Stephanie, he had never imagined it would be in a small town in Arkansas.

He still didn't understand how things had gotten out of hand earlier. Steph was her soft, sweet self one minute and ready to hang him the next. Caught off guard by the site of her, all the things he'd rehearsed over the years had vanished from his mind. He had blown it.

Stephanie was right here in the Ozarks and even more beautiful than he remembered. She was the angel who had haunted his dreams for so long. What he'd meant to do was explain everything that had happened to him these past few years, due in part to her throwing him out. He needed to know what he'd missed in her life. The last time he had seen her, she was saying 'I do' to Matthew Douglas. He had watched from the back of the church as she became another man's wife. Now, years later, she was here of all places. Where was Matthew? What was a beautiful woman like Stephanie doing at this event unescorted? Sure it was business but it wouldn't have prevented Brendan from making sure everyone present knew she belonged only to him.

Beautiful didn't begin to describe the woman who had stood before him earlier. The patio light combined with the light from the chandeliers shining through the tall windows made every rhinestone on her full, dark blue satin gown twinkle like stars. The moonlight played across milky-white shoulders, bared by a thick halo of upswept golden hair.

Brendan shook his head in disgust. He couldn't allow himself to think like that. Stephanie told him in no uncertain terms that he didn't have a chance as long as he was drinking. Except she hadn't waited for him to stop drinking before she had moved on with her life. Brendan rubbed at the back of his neck, trying to release some of the tightness pulling on every nerve in his body.

"Dad? What are you doing out here?" Jennifer slipped an arm around her father.

"Just getting some air, sweetheart. How does it look inside?"

"I'll know more tomorrow. I never add anything until the last person is gone."

"Are you superstitious like your mother?" Brendan grinned, pulling her close.

Jennifer shrugged and leaned against him. "I guess so. Mom always said I was more like you. Do you realize it has been over two years since you've been here? I hope you're not planning another world tour any time soon. I'd really like it if we had a chance to spend some time together."

His daughter's attempt to change the subject didn't go unnoticed by Brendan. They'd never really talked about Debbie's death. Maybe it was for the best. He and Debbie had never been each other's favorite subject alive, talking about her now didn't seem right.

"Not till after the first of the year," Brendan replied.

"Really?"

Her squeal of delight warmed his soul though he couldn't help but remember the times he failed to deliver surprises like this in her younger years. They had mended that fence as best they could, but some things he would never get back.

Brendan laughed. "Really. I've rented a studio in Branson to work on a new album. I can't be on the other side of the world the day my baby gets married now can I?"

Jennifer flung both arms around him. "Dad, that's wonderful!"

"I thought you'd be pleased. But speaking of Branson, I have to make a trip up there tomorrow. Do you want to meet me for dinner?" Brendan asked as they walked back into the hotel, arm in arm.

"Sure. David is on a job site there. I'll call and ask him to meet us at the Rib Shack."

"Great. I need sleep. It's been a very long day. I'll see you tomorrow." Brendan kissed her forehead.

Hoping the exertion of the three-flight climb to his suite might help further ease some of the tension; he chose the stairs over the elevator.

In his room he sat down in an ornate chair and pulled off his boots. Standing to remove his shirt, he caught sight of the picture he took on the road with him. In a silver plated frame on the night table, a blonde with sparkling blue eyes smiled back at him. Stephanie had given it to him for his birthday a couple of months before the break up. He thought back to the first time he'd seen her smile, one of the few solid memories I had of their time together.

It had been a long day on the construction site. Nothing had gone right. The rain began early that morning, a slow and steady drizzle that made his job hazardous. His best framer slipped on wet planking and fell just before lunch. By the time they had gotten out of the emergency room, all Brendan had been able to think about was a beer. Spotting Stephanie the minute he entered the bar quickly put other things on his mind. He ate lunch there nearly every day for six months and had never noticed the petite blonde before.

Stephanie had looked up at the jingling of the bell above the door. Their eyes locked as an invisible current shot between them, connecting their souls

God, he'd missed her over the years. All he wanted to do was make things right. But how was he supposed to do that? Stephanie was married. She had a family that did not include him.

Yanking the shirt off and tossing it across the chair, he turned to the open window of his room overlooking the valley. A warm breeze whispered around him, caressing the smooth bare chest Stephanie once rested her head on as they had cuddled that first cold winter together. Even now, he could still feel the softness of her hair as he filtered the strands through his fingers.

Many times, they'd lain in silence for hours just enjoying each other's company. He knew she wanted to hear him say 'I love you'. How was he supposed to love her and provide her with everything she deserved? He'd been a drunk for as long as he could remember, having had had his first beer at fourteen. From then on, every day of his life gradually became a booze-induced fog. The only times he could recollect even remotely were the ones with Steph.

They had gone to midnight movies. Cold pizza had been the food of choice. Passionate romps were interspersed with games of gin rummy. She always seemed to know what he was thinking, when he needed her and how he felt. And in return, he had forgotten her birthday and used her as well as other women to satisfy his own desires when it suited him. If someone looked up CAD in the dictionary, his picture would smile back at them.

He hadn't realized at the time what he was doing. Much of it he'd remembered through his own counseling and sponsoring others in the program over the years. Through the program he'd learned about the mistakes he made. But Stephanie hadn't been there for him to heal that part of his life.

Gazing out the window, Brendan knew she was there and that she was thinking of him. She had to be. She was so close and he couldn't tell her that he knew what a jerk he had been and how sorry he was. She had a husband who gave her everything he hadn't been able to. Swearing to himself, he went into the bathroom and turned on the shower. It was going to be a very long night.

CHAPTER 2

"Are you okay, Mom?" Kimberly asked, pouring milk on her cereal and filling a cup for Max.

"Sure Hon, I'm fine." Stephanie forced a smile. "Why do you ask?" Actually, her head hurt and her eyes felt as if they were on fire. If only she did not have to open the shop today or see Jennifer.

Kimberly pointed to her mom's bowl, giggling. "Most people use milk on their cereal, not orange juice."

Stephanie looked at the little round O's swimming in the murky orange pool like life preservers before emptying them down the disposal.

"Guess I'm not awake yet." She forced a laugh at her mistake. Truth was, she had not slept much at all.

"Did we make a lot for the Santa Club?"

"I don't have a total yet, but checks were being written when I left. I think we did very well."

"I'll bet it's because of Brendan Keane." The

teenager gushed as she put her bowl in the sink. "He is the hottest guy in country music. Jennifer is so lucky to have him for a dad."

"I would imagine she isn't as lucky as you might think. Jennifer would never have any privacy because of who her father is. Celebrities sacrifice a lot for the spotlight." She thought back to when Jennifer was little and how growing up during her dad's addiction had cost them precious memories.

"Come on, you'll be late for play practice." Stephanie saw the questions already forming in her daughter's mind. Questions she wasn't ready to answer.

"I can't believe we have known Jennifer all this time and she never let on. Do you think she would let me meet him while he's here?" Kimberly asked, putting her jacket on and pulling her thick, dark hair into a clip.

"I don't know Kim. Mr. Keane has a very busy schedule. We were lucky to get him last night. I'm not sure how long he'll be here." Silently she prayed he had already left.

"Oh, well, he'll be here for her wedding. Bye Mom. Remember, I'm going out for pizza with the cast after practice. With that, Kimberly was out the back door.

After setting coffee to drip, she unbuckled Max from his booster chair and helped him to the floor.

"Come on little man." He grasped her finger and they made their way down the front hall to the office. "You can watch your favorite show while I tidy up."

The morning sun streamed in the tall windows,

touching the blush-toned tile of the office, casting a rosy hue to the cream walls. The Chintz covered mahogany settee and chair added to the cozy feeling.

Once used as a parlor in the modestly styled 1882 Victorian, Stephanie used the room for the sole purpose of promoting and tending to the business of planning. Whether a retirement party for ten or a grand wedding for three hundred, Stephanie wanted to be sure that 'Planned to Perfection' presented the grace and charm representative of the community that had accepted her little family two years ago.

With her son settled on the play rug in front of the television, she adjusted the infant gate across the entrance to the hall. His favorite show would occupy him long enough for her to finish up in the kitchen. The tinkling of the bell above the door chimed just as she was putting the carafe of coffee on the tray.

"Hi, Max!" The toddler's laughter carried down the hall. Through the kitchen doorway, Stephanie watched him greet the young woman at the gate, arms raised. Jennifer scooped the chattering little boy up and kissed his cheek.

"Stephanie, you are so lucky. He's such a sweetheart. You get to stay home with him and have a business." She sat the child down and opened the gate for Stephanie.

"It isn't as easy as it sounds." Jennifer unlatched the gate, allowing Stephanie to step through then slipped the latch back in place. "There are days when I know I'd get three times as much done if I didn't have a two year old to cart around. But I wouldn't trade a second of the time we have either."

Stephanie put the tray on the low Queen Anne table and joined Jennifer on the sofa. She poured a cup of coffee for each of them.

"So how did we do last night?"

"We beat last year's total by a thousand dollars! Can you believe it? You always do so well getting people together. Everything went smoothly, as I knew it would, thanks to you. And Dad wrote a check to be earmarked for the start of next year's fund."

Stephanie flinched at the mention of Brendan. "That was nice of your Dad. I'm glad he was able to fit the gala into his busy schedule. Has he gone back out this morning?" She took a hesitant sip of the hot coffee, hoping for an affirmative answer.

"No, he has business in Branson today. David and I are meeting him for dinner. Why don't you join us?"

Her jaw tightened, thankful that Jennifer, in reaching for the creamer, had not noticed her discomfort.

"I don't think so." The china cup rattled in the saucer as she struggled to sit it down

gently. "With the gala behind me, I really need to finish some things here at the shop. I have three weddings over the next three months, one of which is yours. I also have final details for Judge Avery's retirement party. Speaking of weddings, have you and David made any decisions on the guest list yet?" She hoped to change the subject, but her friend would not be detoured.

"That's what I mean. You work all the time. When was the last time you went out just for your own enjoyment?" Jennifer raised her hand, preventing Stephanie from offering any excuses in her own defense. "I don't mean pizza with Kimberly's theater group or the Chamber potluck last week. I mean a real relaxed, unconnected to anything, evening out."

"I just don't have time. My evenings are reserved for the kids when I am not attending one of the events I spend the daytime planning. Besides, you need time with your father. The two of you see so little of one another. When does he leave?"

"Oh, that's the best news of the day." Jennifer's pleasure radiated from her as she sat her cup down and clasped her hands together in obvious delight. "Dad has suspended the beginning of the next tour. He's rented a studio in Branson to work on the new album. He'll be here for all the wedding planning. Isn't that wonderful?"

Stephanie forced a smile as her young friend beamed. Jennifer deserved this time with her father. Even if the choices had been Brendan's to make, his daughter had suffered the most. She never had a dad around for the important things in her life. And although it meant being near him again, Stephanie would get through this for her dearest friend.

"It's good the two of you will get to spend this special time together."

"Finally. I realize he is in demand all the time but Dad and I see each other so little and with Mom gone I just really need him, you know." Jennifer brushed at an unshed tear.

"I know. How is David? I didn't see him at the Gala." Stephanie made another attempt at steering the conversation away from Brendan as she refilled her cup.

"He couldn't get away. They are almost finished with the new amphitheater. They've made some last minute changes he needs to take care of and he's supposed to start on renovations at Silver Dollar City in a couple of weeks. I haven't seen him much the last few days either."

"See, another good reason for me to not go. You need the time with David as much as you do your father." Stephanie reached across to pat her hand. "And it won't get any easier once you're married, so make use of the chances you do get. Trust me, I know." Her voice trailed off as she looked to the small table where Matthew's academy photo sat, as if he were watching over her.

She recalled the number of nights she had not been able to spend with Matthew because of his job as a police officer and now never would. Oh, how she missed him. His death left a deep void in her heart and the life of their children.

Music from the TV signaled the end of the show and Max's attention. He wandered the room in search of new entertainment. Stephanie watched as he made his way on chubby legs to the gated doorway and began throwing his toys into the hall.

The tingling of the bell above the front door announced a client. She heard a heavy thud on the hardwood floor followed by a few choice words. Stephanie hurried to the gate with Jennifer close behind her in time to see Brendan on his back amidst the toys.

"Daddy, are you all right?" Jennifer followed her over the gate, neither bothering to unlock it, and knelt next to Brendan.

"I'm fine. I think this saved me." He pulled a stuffed purple bear from beneath the lower part of his body and handed it back over the gate to Max. "Do all your clients drop in like this Stephanie?"

Stephanie laughed. "Are you sure you're all right? Can you stand?" She offered her hand to help him up.

He looked at her hand for only a brief second before taking it in his own. The current that shot through Stephanie caught her off guard. There had always been a charge with him she failed to have with Matthew. It was like a sparkler you only played with on the Fourth of July.

"This must be the young man you were telling me about." Brendan smiled at Max as he stood, extending a finger to be instantly grasped by the toddler. He picked the delighted boy up and pretended to touch his head to the top of the doorframe. Max giggled at the new game. Stephanie's throat constricted at the picture they made.

"Would you like some coffee, Dad? And there are plenty of croissants left. Steph makes the best peach preserves."

"I'd love some."

Stephanie opened the gate, allowing him to step through. He crossed to a Queen Anne chair by the window, picking up one of Max's books off the floor as he went.

Brendan settled himself on the delicate chair, tucked Max into the crook of his arm, and opened the book.

"I want to thank you again for your contribution both musically and financially to the Santa Club." Stephanie forced a warm, business tone. Not only was this community her safe haven, but so was the business she was building, the fortress she never imagined he'd breach.

Her hand trembled as she poured him a cup of coffee, causing the liquid to slosh over the rim of the delicate china cup into the accompanying saucer. He raised an eyebrow in questions as he motioned for her to set the china on the side table next to him.

"I was glad to do it. I have a strong commitment to charities that involve kids. That is why I founded Keane's Kids. Regardless of their circumstance, they shouldn't have to do without not only the necessities but the pleasures of life as well. When Jennifer called to ask if there was a spot open on the tour, I had to do it. I haven't told her 'no' to much of anything."

"Well, except for the kitten I wanted for my tenth birthday!" Jennifer pouted playfully.

"But you got a puppy for Christmas."

Stephanie remembered that little brown bundle of fur he was referring to. She had spent the entire day with him, shopping for the perfect puppy. They had promised Debbie it would be a small dog with all its shots. No strays allowed. If Debbie had known it came from the local shelter and not a pet store, she would have had fits. Stephanie ventured a smile at Brendan and knew he remembered too.

"You do have a way with children, Dad." Jennifer nodded to the now sleeping boy.

"Guess he was bored with all this grown up talk." Stephanie smiled as she rose to take him from Brendan.

"No, let me." He placed the book on the table then stood, shifting the sleeping toddler to his shoulder. "Lead the way."

Her legs felt like rubber with each step to the second floor bedroom, ever conscious of Brendan's breathing behind her.

"In here." She stepped aside in the doorway to let them pass. "Just lay him on his tummy, he is old enough now and prefers to sleep that way." Just like his father.

Stephanie raised a hand to her mouth in an attempt to cover the pain she knew would come with the memory. Matthew had been gone nearly three years and little things such as Max's sleeping habits still hurt.

"Are you all right, Stephanie?" Brendan placed a hand on her shoulder. "Why did you run out last night? I... we need to talk."

Searching his face, she saw every question he wanted to ask. She had come to read that face and understand so much about this man when no one else seemed to be able to or care. They shared everything once.

Clasping her hands behind her back, she fought the impulse to stroke his cheek, to run a fingertip across the lips she had felt so many times. How could she still want to do that? Hadn't he made the choice by refusing to include her in his life full time? She squeezed her eyes tight, struggling to hold back tears.

"Steph, talk to me, please," Brendan's voice barely a whisper as he moved his hand from her shoulder to the side of her face.

"Oh Brendan." She couldn't stop the agony in her voice. Having him so close, to touch her in such a tender way pierced her soul. "Why did it have to be your Jennifer? I don't want you here. Don't you realize how much it took to get you out of my life and my heart?"

"Am I really out of your heart, Steph?"

The landline phone she kept strictly for business, rang in the office and she seized the opportunity. Turning, she hurried back down the stairs, not noticing whether or not he followed. Jennifer met her in the hall.

"I took a message and left it on the blotter for you, Steph. I need to get back to the hotel."

"Do you want a ride up there?" Brendan offered.

Stephanie watched him retrieve his keys from a pocket of the molded jeans. How was there room for his hand, let alone anything else the compartment might hold?

"I have my car. Bye Steph. I promise to have the guest list to you before the first of the week." Jennifer hugged her tight then turned to Brendan. "We'll see you for dinner tonight. Eight o'clock okay? David will work right up to dusk."

"That's fine." Brendan held the door to allow his daughter to leave before turning back to Stephanie.

"It was nice to see you, angel."

And Brendan Keane was gone, again. But this time, she knew he would be back. And he would want answers. She prayed he would be able to accept the only ones she could give.

She went back into the office to collect the dishes. There wasn't time to think about him right now. She had a business to run. Days were short enough in which to accomplish her tasks without adding Brendan, and the past, to her list.

* * *

Brendan watched his daughter play with her straw, stirring it around in the soda glass. As they sat in the Rib Shack waiting for David, she began the grilling he had anticipated. After witnessing the scene at the hotel last night Jennifer wanted answers.

"Okay, Dad, out with it. How do you know Stephanie?"

He studied his daughter. He had not spent near enough time with her over the years, particularly since Debbie's illness and death. The concert tours, recording sessions, movie deals all kept him busy. They were more of an excuse and he knew it. Having not been allowed to spend time with Jennifer as she grew up made it easy for Brendan to convince himself she didn't need him as an adult either.

Jennifer the little girl had blossomed into a beautiful, young woman. Debbie did a great job in raising her. Thanks to Stephanie, he had even managed to be a minuscule part of her life for a while.

It was Stephanie who called Debbie and got the go ahead for the puppy when Jennifer was ten. She was the one to insist he go shopping so his parents could take presents by for birthdays. And now in a strange twist of fate, it was Jennifer bringing her back into his life. He strongly believed everything happened for a reason.

"Dad, hello." She waved a hand in front of his face. "I want details."

He sighed, took a long drink of his iced tea then looked across the table at his daughter. Though twenty-five, she still reminded him of the little girl in ponytails.

"It was a long time ago, Jennifer."

"A lot of things were a long time ago. So what happened? Did Stephanie have something to do with you and Mom not getting together? Is she the reason you weren't around much when I was growing up?"

"Don't blame her, Jennifer!" He scrubbed his face with his hands. He hadn't meant to speak so sharply. Thankfully their booth was in the corner, providing privacy for what had the makings of a very spicy dinner.

"I'm sorry. I'm just… "

"Just what, Dad?"

"Stephanie would have walked away from us a lot sooner than she did if it meant I had a chance to raise you. She loved kids and tried everything to see what I was missing in your life." Brendan leaned against the back of the booth, fiddling with his spoon before continuing.

"No, she came along after all the stuff between your mother and me. You were about nine when I met her. She is eight years younger than I am, being only seventeen when we met. I wanted her the first moment our eyes met across that restaurant. I was drunk, she was young; it was perfect." He tossed the spoon onto the table in frustration.

Jennifer motioned for the waitress to refill their drinks. "So what happened?"

"We had a thing for about three years. Nothing steady, just if I was around or she needed a place to get away from her father. Remember, those were my drunken days. I treated her like garbage. She loved me but I didn't have my priorities in order. I didn't have room for anyone or anything that didn't come in a can. She was always there when I needed her though."

He paused, spooning sugar into his tea. "I remember when your Uncle Steve got killed in a boating accident. She wouldn't let me drink. I don't know how, but she kept me sober and got me through the funeral. Your Grandpa thought she was a peach."

"So who broke it off?"

"Stephanie. She wanted a home and kids. I just wasn't ready to give her that, no matter how I felt about her." He picked up his spoon and began stirring his tea again, watching the whirlpool it created in the clear plastic glass, pulling the ice cubes to the bottom. Just like the booze had done to his life all those years ago.

"It happened a couple days after her birthday. I had gotten drunk and forgot to pick her up or even call."

Jennifer's phone buzzed.

"It's David. I'm going to step outside and call him. I'll be right back." She slid out of the booth and started to walk towards the door. She stopped and turned to look at him. "We're not through with this conversation."

Brendan took a drink of his tea and looked out the window at the Strip. The tourist traffic knotted like the emotions inside him as he thought back to that day. Funny how some things had left his mind, yet one look at that heart-shaped face and he remembered a conversation like it was this morning. God, he had been so stupid!

Over pizza, she told him about meeting Matthew. They had been seeing quite a bit of one another.

"Brendan, I love you and a part of me probably always will but I want more. Matthew has asked me to marry him."

"Are you sure?" Brendan asked, already taking a last swallow of his beer and heading for the door.

"Sometimes I think yes and other times no, but I'm tired of waiting for you to get it together and decide where we belong. I'm sorry Brendan, but I can't wait anymore."

Those were the last words he remembered them speaking. Now she was planning his daughter's wedding. So lost in the memory, he was startled by the sound of Jennifer's voice as she sat back in the booth.

"The inspector is due early in the morning and they have some things to finish up. He asked if we'd just make sure he had leftovers."

The waitress chose that moment to place a large platter of baby back ribs layered with gooey barbecue sauce.

"I think there will be if this platter of ribs is any indication."

Brendan filled his plate with meat as well as potato salad from a large bowl before asking his question.

"So tell me, how long has Stephanie been down here?"

"Nearly three years. They moved down right after Max was born. He'll turn three Thanksgiving."

"What does Matthew do? Is he on the police department?"

Brendan froze as the rib bone Jennifer had been eating from fell to her plate, her eyes widening in astonishment. "You don't know."

"Know what?"

"Matthew was shot while on patrol just over two years ago, leaving her to bring Max into this world on her own and raise both he and his sister without a father."

He paused with his fork in midair, letting his brain register what she had told him. Matthew was dead. Brendan asked the only question that raced through his mind.

"Has she remarried?"

"Dad!" She wiped her hands on a napkin then took a drink of soda. "No. From what Steph has told me she and Matthew really had something special. And those two kids are proof. Max is the most adorable little boy. It's a shame Matthew never got to see him.

"What about her daughter, Kimberly isn't it?"

"Kimberly is warm and compassionate like her mother. I'm sure she's had to grow up a lot in the last couple of years. She's a big help with Max while Stephanie runs the business."

"I haven't met her yet. How old is she?" By now Brendan had lost his appetite. He pushed his plate back and motioned for the waitress to box the rest.

"Kimberly turned twelve in June."

So that was why she married Matthew. He had gotten her pregnant and she needed a father she could depend on for her child. Brendan took a drink of tea, realizing he just needed some air. He took out his wallet and removed a credit card.

"Do you mind if we don't take in a movie? I'm really beat."

"Not at all. You've hardly had time to catch your breath since getting in yesterday."

Reaching into her purse, she pulled out a folded piece of paper and handed it to her father. "Will you go over this guest list and either get it back to me or drop it by Steph's in the next day or two?" She picked up her belongings and the takeout box.

"Sure." Anything that would give him a valid reason to see her again.

Out in the parking lot, they stopped beside Jennifer's car. He waited while she unlocked the door and got in before saying anything further.

"Jennifer?"

"Yeah, Dad?"

"Stephanie is a good person. Don't judge her on things that happened between the two of us. You've made a good friend in her. Hang on to that and plan the biggest wedding Eureka Springs has ever seen. If there is anything for Stephanie and I to resolve, it's between us, okay?"

Brendan forced a smile he didn't feel as his thoughts zoomed like race cars on a track. His mind refused to put order to the questions. He hadn't planned on Stephanie being a widow. His plan when he saw her was always to apologize for being a jerk and hope she accepted. Now his mind conjured up a different scenario.

"I still have questions, I'm just not sure what they are yet. Steph and I have been good friends and we work together. There's a lot I don't know about her apparently. You do what you have to Dad. I'm here if you need to talk."

"How'd you get so smart?" He tapped her nose and grinned. "Watch the curves going home."

She waved before putting the red Neon into gear and pulling out into a break in the Branson traffic.

Brendan walked towards his car then thought better of it. He was not ready to go back to the hotel. In fact, he would probably end up on the front step of Stephanie's gingerbread-trimmed Victorian pounding on the door if he went back now. And he did not want to do that. At least not until he was ready to face whatever answers Stephanie might give him.

At this point, he was not even sure what all the questions were. He did know that she still had to be the most beautiful woman he had ever met, and there had been a lot of them. But none had touched his soul like Stephanie—his angel.

He had messed things up once. If there was to be a second chance, Brendan knew he had to know all the questions and have the answers before making any decisions. He'd gotten sober one step at a time. He would win Stephanie's love the same way.

The first step was to relax and clear his head. Music would do that. Without further thought, he walked up the street to one of the clubs. A good round on the drums ought to help. He had gotten his break playing in the clubs here. And there was a standing invitation throughout the strip to drop by any time. Tonight, he would take one of them up on it.

CHAPTER 3

Brendan wandered aimlessly around Stephanie's office, his handcrafted boots making little sound on the tile floor. Fingering various items displayed throughout the room, he looked for anything that might fill in the years.

The last time he'd seen Stephanie had been on her wedding day. He'd slipped into the church just after the ceremony began and left before the kiss. Watching another man taste the sweetness would have been too much, even for his booze-numbed soul. Though he'd been sober for a few months at that point, he didn't remember a lot of things until someone flipped a memory switch. The day she'd married Matthew, Brendan had sworn to stay out of her life and he had - until now.

Last night in Branson, J.C. took one look at Brendan's face and knew what brought his friend to the club. Having been one of the first club owners in the area to hire him all those years ago, there wasn't much about him the entertainer didn't know. That included his feelings for Stephanie.

Before the final show began J.C. had handed him the sticks and let him slip behind the drums unbeknownst to the crowded auditorium. For two hours, he hadn't been Brendan Keane, superstar. Being just the drummer in the backlit stage he'd felt more himself than he had in a long time.

During the drive back to Eureka Springs in the pre-dawn hours, he'd been able to think more clearly. Stephanie was still the love of his life. Matthew was gone. She had the two kids to think about and he was well into recovery. It was time to move ahead - for all of them.

Now he stood glancing through a collection of photos on a Queen Anne pedestal table. Some of the faces he recognized. An ornate white frame stood off-center amongst the group. Stephanie in her wedding gown beamed from the picture. Matthew in a black tux with a deep blue cummerbund stood next to her. The photographer had created an ethereal background, adding to their magical day. Brendan couldn't bring himself to touch the frame. Being at the wedding, watching them had been hard. He saw their happiness more clearly now and he ached for the pain she must carry with her.

An oak frame stood next to their wedding photo. With hesitant fingers, Brendan reached for the frame. The perfect family smiled back at him. Matthew, out of uniform, knelt in the grass with an arm draped around Stephanie and Kimberly on either side of him. This is what she had wanted; the life he'd been unable to give her.

Gently he replaced the photo, feeling as if he'd intruded, and looked around the room radiating with her touch. A love for the bygone era was prominent throughout the room. The mix of printed fabrics and colors reflected Stephanie - soft, warm and welcoming. The deep Mahogany Victorian furnishings portrayed her sensibility and strength. All the things he loved about her.

"OMG!"

Brendan turned towards the doorway to meet the stare from eyes the size and color of chocolate drops. He smiled in amusement and ventured to speak. "Hi there, you must be Kimberly." He walked towards her, stopped and watched the blush creep over her young face.

"I...um, yeah that's me."

Brendan grinned at the nervous young lady before him. She resembled Stephanie only slightly. Where Steph's hair was warm autumn gold, Kimberly's was much darker and her skin a natural tan in contrast to her mother's fairness. Her petite size and heart-shaped face is where the likeness began and ended. He watched as she twirled a finger in her shoulder-length hair, just like his own daughter did when she was nervous.

"Mom's upstairs tending to Max. Would you like me to get her?"

"No that's fine. I'll wait if that's okay?"

"Sure. May I get you some ice tea or something?" She was already backing slowly to the doorway, never taking her eyes from him.

"I'd love a glass, thanks." He wouldn't laugh but he couldn't resist flashing his best smile as she twirled her hair tighter.

"I'll be right back." Kimberly turned and fled the room, just missing the doorframe in her hasty retreat.

The teenager had barely left when he poked his head out into the hall to wiggle his fingers in a wave. Drawing on experience with fans, he knew she would stop just out of sight to collect herself. She answered his wave then walked quickly to the kitchen.

Brendan's laughter reverberated through the hall, shaking Stephanie all the way to her toes. She'd witnessed his teasing wave from her spot on the upper landing. So much like the man she remembered. He'd always been a tease and a flirt but she'd also known a quiet side most people had never seen. Brendan really would have been great with kids if only he'd made the right choices sooner.

Slowly, she made her way down the stairs to her office. Brendan stood, thumbs hooked in the back pockets of his jeans, looking out the window. He turned at the sound of her heeled shoes as she entered the room.

"Hello, Steph."

"What brings you by? I thought you were finalizing plans on the recording studio."

Stephanie sat down at her desk and began shuffling papers. There wasn't anything in particular she needed, but she couldn't look at him without falling under his devilish spell. The attraction to him had been too much for her to resist until Matthew became her shield. Now he was gone and she had only her own defenses to rely on.

"I won't actually get into the studio before the end of the week. Besides, it's Sunday. Don't you ever take a day off?"

There was that smile. The one that had captured her heart across the pool table a lifetime ago. She would not fall for his wiles again. There was too much at stake.

"I have a business to run and a family to raise. I have to make full use of my quiet time," she said pointedly.

"Well, I just needed to drop this off." He tossed what she recognized as the guest list onto the desk.

"Thank you. I'll get it over to the calligrapher in the morning."

"Why didn't you tell me, Steph?" His voice was almost inaudible.

"Tell... tell you what?" She fumbled with items on her desk, refusing to look up. How did he know? Was it that obvious?

"About Matthew." He strode around to her side of the desk and braced his hip against the edge.

The faded jeans pulled tighter against his muscled thigh. A fleeting memory of those taunt legs entangled with hers amidst satin sheets assisted in making breathing difficult.

Without even realizing she'd held it, Stephanie let out a shaky breath. Matthew! He'd found out about Matthew's death.

"Here's your tea, Mr. Keane." Neither heard Kimberly enter the room. "I brought you one too, Mom."

"Thank you, Kimberly, but my friends call me Brendan." He winked as he took the glass.

"Really! Wow! I mean, I can? Cool! Mom, can I go over to Becky's? Please." She pleaded, never taking her eyes from Brendan. "This is like too outrageous news for the phone."

Stephanie smiled over the rim of the glass at her daughter's adolescent exuberance. His special magic worked on women of any age.

"Go ahead. Be back in time for supper. We have a club meeting and your job is to watch Max, remember?"

"I know, I will. Thanks Mom, bye...Brendan." And she was out the door.

Brendan laughed before saying, "That's some girl, Steph."

"Yes, she is." Stephanie stood, walked over to the sofa, and sat down. "She and Max are the light of my life. I don't know how I'd have gotten through Matthew's death or since without them." She rolled the tall, cool glass back and forth between her palms.

At first, her daughter had been devastated at losing her father, but once the reality of being a big sister set in, living became easier.

A visit to Doc Brady confirmed what Stephanie had suspected a few weeks following the funeral. She carried a lasting part of Matthew, but the stress of losing her husband had nearly taken it away. Doc suggested she needed some time to come to terms with everything and let the baby settle in. Otherwise, he'd warned, she'd be in for a very rough time. Having known the fatherly man seemingly forever, it came as no surprise when he'd dropped the keys to his cabin in Arkansas on the desk in front of her.

After a week at Beaver Lake, Stephanie knew this was where the three of them needed to start over. The atmosphere soothed her wounded soul and the Ozark countryside emulated heaven on earth.

"Tell me what happened."

She was aware of Brendan sitting next to her as she stared into her glass as if it were a crystal ball. But there wasn't anything there that would give her words and strength to say them. Taking a drink of the tea, she sat the glass on the table. Rising, she pressed her cream linen trouser legs smooth before sliding her hands into the pockets. Trance like, she walked to the window.

The late September sun streamed through the pane, warming her face. It replaced some, but not all, of the chill that seeped into her soul whenever she recalled the night she'd gotten the news.

After having relived the nightmare repeatedly in her mind the past three years, it never seemed to hurt any less. Stephanie steeled herself against the anguish she knew would come with the telling.

"Matthew loved being a cop just like his father. And his uncle had been head of the department for years. I wasn't crazy about his job, what wife would be? As a wife, though, it's a lesson I learned early. Being a cop wasn't a job; it's who he was." Stephanie drew a ragged breath as she continued.

"The love and caring he brought to the people on his beat was part of what I fell in love with. There wasn't a person on his patrol that he didn't know. I guess that's why I fooled myself into thinking he'd always be safe." A sob escaped past the armor. "Everyone liked him."

"So what went wrong?"

She was aware of his presence before he settled his hands on her shoulders. She steeled herself against the warmth and security those hands had given her once. She took a cleansing breath then continued.

"We'd been on vacation all week. The three of us had just gotten back from his folks' cabin up by Lake Freeman. We went up there every year. We'd barely unpacked the car when the station called needing him to fill in on a south end patrol. I couldn't understand why he'd work a rough beat if he didn't have to. He was still on vacation and wasn't required to go in."

Brendan's thumbs began a slow pressure at the base of her neck. The sensations that rippled through her gave her the strength to continue.

"Apparently an officer covered for Matthew one night so he could attend Kimberly's final dance recital of the season. He missed a lot of the evening activities because he always seemed to be on night patrol when special events came around. He hadn't wanted to miss this one. He had a chance to return the favor and took it. That was Matthew."

She leaned back against the strength of Brendan's chest and closed her eyes.

"He hadn't even been on a call." She didn't try to stop the flow of tears. Instead, she wrapped her arms tightly around her waist as if protecting the life he had left behind.

"It was around midnight and he was doing door checks. Coming around a corner, he surprised a sixteen year old kid crawling out of a liquor store window."

Reality struck with the force of lightning in that instant. The air crackled with the sudden stillness, quiet before the storm. She pushed away from Brendan, whirling on him as tears streamed down her face. She stared at him, trembling. Her fists clenched so tight she felt her nails bite into the palms of her hands.

"Why Brendan?" She cried. "What is it about alcohol that is so intriguing? Why is it so important that it has to cost a person everything? My kids don't have a father because some punk thought it was cool." She swiped at the tears… angry tears. "And it cost 'us'."

Alcohol had taken the two most important men in her life. The beer Brendan wouldn't give up is what she'd based her decisions on all those years ago. And it was the booze that took Matthew's life, depriving Kimberly and Max of their father. Her father had been another casualty. She'd never seen the attraction.

With arms of steel, tempered with love, he gathered her close, holding her while she cried. She didn't fight him. Being held while she let the pain flow felt right. She hadn't had anyone to hold her when Matthew died.

As the storm within her gradually subsided the sobs became less intense until, in exhaustion, her arms slid around his waist and the tears became nothing more than an occasional hiccup. With one arm still holding her, he stroked her hair with the other hand. All the while whispering consoling words she barely heard.

After several minutes, she raised her tear-streaked face to his. Without hesitation he bent his head, brushing his lips to hers briefly before claiming them fully. In all their time together she couldn't remember this tenderness from him. She knew that Brendan. This man was someone she wished he'd been then.

He broke the kiss first, but continued to watch her. Taking her by the hand, he led her to the desk chair. As if dealing with a child he took a tissue from the box and kneeling before her, began wiping away the tears.

"You can't let it destroy you, angel. I learned the hard way that life goes on. But you have to help. You can't do that by burying yourself in work and the kids. They need you, yes. But you need you."

She listened to his words and knew he was right but she didn't know how. Kimmie and Max had been the foundation of her salvation. Needing to provide for them. They were her world.

"You have to allow yourself time to heal and grow. You're like a tree, Stephanie. You're the roots of this family. If you allow yourself to wither, all the leaves that depend on you for nourishment will fall. But you will have died first. Think about it." Brendan reached up and touched her cheek with the back of his fingers.

"I lived those demons, too, Steph. They stole parts of me that I can never have back. I'm learning to deal with that and I can help you do the same. I'm a call away if you need me." He brushed a kiss to her forehead, turned and left.

* * *

Stephanie wasn't sure how long she'd been sitting in the same chair he'd led her to. Following his calm and silent exit, she had broken into another wave of tears. How could he tell her life went on? He didn't know the gut-wrenching anguish she'd felt the night the Captain had come knocking on her door with the news of her husband's death.

There'd been no time to stand beside a hospital bed in a dismal intensive care unit and hold his hand. No chance to whisper words of hope and encouragement to a man she'd sworn to spend the rest of her life with. There'd been no hospital bed at all. Instead, she'd seen him for the first time just hours before the chapel had been flooded with people offering condolences.

"Stephanie, my God! Are you all right?" Jennifer dropped her briefcase in the doorway and hurried to kneel in front of her.

She failed to hear the tingling of the bell above the front door to know anyone had come in until Jennifer spoke. Stephanie raised her head to meet her friend's worried gaze. If how she felt was any indication, Steph was sure she looked a fright. Hurriedly wiping at the remains of tears, she attempted a reassuring smile before answering.

"I'm okay Jen. Just a little healing in progress." She reached for a tissue, her sights resting on the invitation list as she did so. Jennifer followed her gaze and reached for the paper.

"Dad's been here. Steph, what is going on? This is the second time in three days I've found you in tears because of Dad. It is because of him, isn't it?" She stood and tossed the paper back onto the desk.

Stephanie closed her eyes, leaning her head against the back of the chair, massaging her temples as she did so.

"It's not 'because' of him, Jen." It wasn't. She'd also realized since his visit that it was how she still felt about him that sent her into tears.

That day in the apartment all those years ago, she hadn't told him it was over because she didn't love him but more because she did.

She had met Matthew at a local café where she had picked up a second job in hopes of earning enough money to buy a car. He and his partner came in almost daily for lunch. She learned early that not all police officers ate donuts and drank coffee. Matthew preferred their house salad topped with slices of grilled chicken and drank iced tea or water with his meal. She chatted with him as she did all of her customers but found herself hanging out at his end of the counter each time he came in. She smiled remembering he had taken almost a month to get enough courage to ask her out. She had been hesitant at first but was slowly realizing Brendan was not going to change.

She ended their third date in tears after finding out she was pregnant. In the front seat of his truck, Matthew had gathered her in his arms, assuring her everything would be okay. A calmness like she had never experienced washed over her and she believed what he said to be true. The next day he had shown up at the café with a dozen yellow roses and proposed in front of everyone. She couldn't say no nor did she want to. Someone loved her, and wanted to love the life she carried. Her 'yes' had been a fresh start.

She had loved Matthew almost from the beginning. As their relationship grew, she understood the difference in what she felt for Brendan and what she shared with her husband. Though a part of her had always wondered 'what if', she had never regretted her time with Matthew. He had been a superb dad to Kimberly and would have loved Max equally.

As if through telepathy, they heard her youngest chattering in his room through the monitor. She sighed in exhaustion and in relief at not having to answer Jennifer's question.

"You stay put, I'll get him. Then I'll make us some herbal tea. You look as if you could use a cup."

After Jennifer left the room, Stephanie walked over to where the tea glasses still sat, barely touched and carried them out to the kitchen. She couldn't 'just sit' as Jennifer instructed. If she didn't continue to move, she feared crumbling again. There wasn't time for that. In some aspects, he was right - life did go on.

Rinsing the glasses out and placing them in the dishwasher was a mindless task yet it took everything she could muster not to drop one. Why did the most important element of the fundraiser have to be 'her Brendan'? This was her haven - a sanctuary to raise her children. But who was going to protect her from the devilish enigma that was Brendan Keane?

Stephanie drummed her short nails on the counter edge as she recalled how good he looked. She still felt the intake of breath and the quickening beat of her heart when she looked into those twinkling eyes. It had taken every ounce of strength earlier not to run her fingers through the short layers of hair above and behind his ears. She remembered that softness every time her fingers touched the black rabbit in Max's touch and feel book. He'd always been particular about his appearance to the point of being almost vain. 'He had a reputation to uphold,' he'd proclaimed back then.

Well, now he had a reputation of a different kind. He still had to present the illusion of being the ladies man. That's what sold albums and concert tickets. But he wasn't cocky about it now. She wondered if the playboy image had gone down the drain with his last can of beer.

The teakettle whistled, Jennifer came into the kitchen chattering with Max, and Kimberly slammed the front screen. The tidal wave of sounds crashed against her strained nerves. She jumped, dropping the cup she'd just taken from the cupboard, sending shards of china across the kitchen tile.

"Wow Mom! Are you okay?" Kimberly asked, stopping abruptly in the kitchen doorway.

Stephanie struggled to keep the tears in check, biting the inside of her lower lip, tasting the saltiness of blood.

"Your mom's just had a hard day, Kim." Jennifer stood Max down onto the floor. "There's a new Disney movie in my briefcase for you guys. Why don't you take your brother into the office while I help your mom clean up?"

"Sure Jennifer. Come on Squirt. Let's go watch a movie." Kimberly led him down the hall.

Stephanie collapsed into a chair, burying her face in her hands. There were no tears, just an attempt at bringing some peace to her shredded soul. She was aware of her friend sweeping up remains of the china cup and taking another from the cabinet. Only after Jennifer placed a steaming cup of tea before her, did Stephanie look up?

"Want to tell me what's going on?" Jennifer spooned honey into her tea before handing the earthenware crock across to Steph.

"Oh Jennifer, I don't even know where to start."

"How about with why every time my dad comes around, I find you in tears.

She attempted a weak smile. "I'm sure you know by now that your dad and I didn't just meet at the gala."

"He told me that you two had some fun together in the old days and that you sent him packing after you met Matthew."

She sat silently for a moment, watching Jennifer. There was a hint of bitterness in her voice. Steph could see the princess coming to her father's defense. Taking a sip of the hot tea, she gently set the cup back onto the saucer before looking to Jennifer, her voice soft and even.

"I didn't "send him packing' really. At the time he was the center of my universe. But a can of beer was the center of his. After almost three years, I couldn't deal with that any longer. For as much as I loved him, I hated what he was refusing to see."

"What was that?"

"That he loved me. There were things I wanted that your dad wasn't ready to provide. Matthew was. We shared the same goals in life and I truly loved him"

"So what about dad, didn't you love him?"

"Did I ever. I'd have given almost anything to spend my life with him. Unfortunately, he wasn't ready to spend his with any one person. Alcohol had been a part of his life for so long that I didn't see a future for us regardless of how much I loved him."

"But he did quit drinking. "He hasn't touched a drop in nearly twelve years."

"I know. Giving up the booze was a tough decision. I was so proud of him when your grandpa told me." Steph smiled fondly at the thought of Brendan's dad.

"You know Pop?"

"When your dad and I broke up I didn't leave the family." She took another drink of her tea then continued. "Your Aunt Kris and I stayed in contact as did your grandparents. I think your grandpa always hoped we'd work things out. Did you know he's the one who gave me away when I got married?"

"He did! Why? Where was your dad?"

"Buried in a bottle. He didn't even come to the wedding. I'm not sure if he even realized it was my wedding day. When dad got to drinking, I stayed away."

"Stephanie, I'm so sorry." Jennifer reached across the pine tabletop to touch her friend's hand. "Did Dad come to the wedding?"

She shook her head. "I sent him an invitation. I know it might seem tacky, but I really wanted him there as a friend. I didn't have a lot of those back then." Stephanie stood and took her cup and saucer to the dishwasher.

"Why didn't you tell me you knew Dad?"

"A lot of reasons. Partly, I guess, because of who your dad is. I didn't want you to think I'm some kind of a groupie or something." Stephanie smiled, attempting to lighten the mood.

"Do you love my dad now?"

The question came as a whisper. Stephanie stilled. The answer she wanted to give scared her to death. Her friendship with this woman was important. She couldn't lie to her. Quietly, she shut the dishwasher and faced Jennifer, hands in her pockets.

"I don't think I ever stopped. There's a part of me that will always belong to him, just as there's a part that's reserved for Matthew."

"Mom, the movie's over."

"Heavens!" Stephanie looked at the clock on the microwave. "The Art Club will be here in less than an hour and I haven't done a thing. Why don't we get the dining room set up? After everyone's here, we'll order out for pizza."

"Sounds like a plan." Jennifer got up and came around the table to hug Steph.

"I'm going to tell you the same thing I told Dad." She stepped back, looking Stephanie in the eyes. "I love you both and I'm not getting in the middle. Just so you know I'm here if you need anything."

"That means a lot Jen. I never thought I'd have to confront all these feelings again. After today, I think I'm better prepared." She smiled at Jennifer. So much like the little girl she'd first met all those years ago and yet so mature. "You are a lot like him, you know." She took hold of Jennifer's hands. "You have grown into an incredible young woman and I'm glad to call you my friend."

"Mom, we're hungry." Kimberly bound into the kitchen, Max running along behind.

"Why don't you fix a peanut butter sandwich and some milk? That'll hold you till everyone gets here. Then we'll order pizza. We're going to get the dining room ready."

"Okay."

She looked from Kimberly to Jennifer, noticing for the first time how strong a resemblance there was between the two. How long would it be before he noticed? The time would come when she would have to tell him the secret she'd kept for years.

CHAPTER 4

The grizzled old man stood at the far length of the rough-hewn oak table. Cottony gray hair encircled his head like a silver halo, the length of it falling unevenly just below his ears. Crystal blue eyes twinkled with pride and merriment in his weathered, leather-tan face. Sparse sideburns made their way down either side of his face, spreading to a full Brillo beard, trailing unevenly to his chest. Dressed in a worn blue flannel shirt and overalls, Whiskers Dan looked every bit the part of Ozarks history.

A kind soul of seventy, he lived in a cabin nestled in a draw above Beaver Lake. A simple four room log structure, it looked the same as it had the day his Pa had finished building their home. That was the fall before Whiskers was born.

Now the old man came into town every day, tools in a little cart in his truck. He pulled the cart around town, spending the day doing handyman repairs for the locals. During the tourist season he spent a lot of time in Basin Park entertaining passersby with his woodwork or a story.

He spent much of his time at the cabin working on projects such as the many toys he created for the Santa Club. A sampling of those he now lovingly showed the group of students gathered in the dining room.

Each toy was made of pine, modeled after ones he'd either played with as a child or designed himself. Every car, truck and doll cradle had the year burned into the bottom as well as his signature 'Whiskers". The toys were a treasure. Stephanie's eyes misted slightly knowing the joy each held for the children. His vision and talent were immeasurable, just as the love he carved into each toy. He truly was Santa Claus.

The five high school girls admired the intricate carving of the cradles and doll chairs. "Vroom, vroom" and "choo, choo" resounded from their four male classmates as they pushed the racecars or train engines across the tabletop. The magic he carved into each toy infected children of any age.

"Hey, Miss Stephanie." Alan, the founding member of the toy division called to her from the far side of the room. "Do you think we have enough cradles? Mrs. McCall said the girl count is up this year."

"We have plenty, Alan. Although we do have more girls, not all will ask for dolls or require cradles."

Mrs. McCall was the secretary at the grade school. As a Santa Club member, it was her job to provide the committee with tentative numbers for Santa visits. Through class registrations and screenings, she was able to provide the Santa Club with invaluable information. Those numbers helped ensure that no child went without at least one gift at Christmas.

"Have you guys set a date to get the painting done and recruited elves?" Stephanie walked around the table, admiring some of the toys.

"Yeah. There's a family day scheduled for the first Saturday in November." One of the girls answered. "The Pep Squad's going to baby-sit in the school gym while the older kids and parents take over the shop department."

"Great. What about lunch? It's an all-day affair."

"Covered." Alan popped up. "The Booster Club is providing chili and stuff. Hey speaking of food, where's the pizza?"

As if on cue, footsteps sounded on the pine steps leading to the porch. The tingling of the bell on the door announced their visitor.

"Anyone order pizza?" Brendan, laden with several pizza boxes balanced in one hand and a case of sodas in the other, entered the hallway.

Everyone turned to stare at the new delivery man. Stephanie giggled as she looked from one astonished face around the table to another. The boys were speechless as they looked at Brendan then to her questioningly. She wasn't sure if the girls needed bibs or smelling salts.

"Dad, how'd you get the pizzas?" Jennifer came around the table to take the boxes.

"I'd stopped in for supper when I overheard the manager yell for delivery. He said something about getting these to the Santa Club meeting. I checked the name on the ticket while I was standing there then persuaded the manager to let me deliver them. Had to tip the regular delivery boy very well, I might add."

The room became a flourish of new activity. Someone cleared a space on the sideboard for the pizzas. Stephanie went into the kitchen for glasses of ice. Brendan pulled the chair with Max's booster seat up to the table before putting the boy in and buckling him safely. Kimberly got paper plates and napkins around to everyone.

Stephanie watched her daughter hold two plates, putting pizza on each and taking one to Brendan. He smiled as he said something and Kimberly laughed. They moved off to sit in the window seat, sitting mirror fashion, munching on the pizza.

It appeared to Stephanie that they were having a contest. As she watched, each of them in turn took a bite, pulling the slice away to see how far the cheese would string before breaking. She recalled a similar game she'd played with Brendan a long time ago. Those contests always ended in one retrieving the broken strands seductively from the other's chin, their pizza abandoned for other adventures.

Brendan chose that moment to look her direction. He stilled momentarily before popping the last bite into his mouth. Had he remembered too? She doubted it. Chances are it was one of the many moments they shared that only she would recall. Max's napkin fluttered to the floor. Picking it up, she wiped the sauce from the tip of his nose.

"I noticed you haven't fixed a plate yet." Brendan's husky voice dusted against her neck. She turned to find herself in very close proximity to her constant distraction. The man was stealth like a lion stalking its prey.

"I...I'm not hungry." Her mouth felt dry and her tongue entirely too large. Chewing food would be impossible at best. Anxiously, she glanced around to see if anyone noticed her position. Whiskers shot her a toothy grin and winked.

She sidestepped Brendan in an attempt to breathe. What a scene they must present for the youth around the table. This was not the time or the place for a make-out session. And Lord how she'd enjoy that--maybe too much.

"Dad." Jennifer tapped him on the shoulder. "The boys want to show you the handiwork before they pack up everything."

"Oh, okay sweetheart." Turning to Stephanie he added, "I'll be back." She took it as a warning.

As Brendan made his way across to Whiskers and the students, she became all too aware of the crowded dining room. His sauntering movement suddenly made the air seem very warm.

"It's written all over your face Steph."

"What?" She struggled not to fan herself. It was October – not warm at all, yet it felt like July.

"That you still love my father. It's okay Steph."

"Seeing your dad again has brought back a lot of memories."

She looked past Jennifer to Brendan. Picking up one of the racecars, he turned it over and around in his large hands. Her heart quickened, remembering the ecstasy those hands evoked.

They were the hands of an artist and when it

came to lovemaking, Brendan was a Picasso. She shut her eyes briefly against the direction her thoughts traveled. When she opened them again, she still continued to watch him.

As he examined the detailing, spinning the wheels with his fingers, Brendan talked with Whiskers and the students. He said something and Whiskers nodded, pointing to the underside of the car.

"Maybe they aren't just memories Steph." Jen continued to stand behind her.

"That's all they can be."

Even with knowing that truth, she still felt her insides turn to jelly whenever he was near. Over the years she'd been able to put her feelings for him aside, like mementos in a box on a shelf. But in reaching for a new start, she'd brought the box and all its memories tumbling around her.

Soon she'd have to deal with the mess. He'd been tucked away in the recesses of her mind for so many years. Seeing the actual vision stride toward her now reminded her of an old Billy Ray tune. Her heart and reality were two different entities.

"Quite a group." Brendan glanced back over his shoulder. "These kids are really on top of things. Whiskers said he enjoys working with them."

"They're very good at this. We're only into our third year." She smiled fondly at the young people filling the small dining room.

One of the older boys, Alan, was the star center for the basketball team and the coordinator for this task force. Within days of the mission statement hitting the local paper, volunteers appeared from everywhere. He'd been the first student.

She learned later that his home life hadn't been very stable over the years. She felt he might have been one of those kids who'd not been able to enjoy the benefits of the Santa Club.

That might explain why this shy, athletic youth poured his heart into the project. And he knew which of his classmates was capable of the same. He'd chosen well and she praised him and the rest of the group many times for their hard work and dedication.

Jennifer joined them as the teenagers began to slide the chairs away from the table and help him pack the toys away.

"I think I'll head home, Dad. The others are starting to leave as well. Do you want some help cleaning up?"

"Go on ahead sweetheart. I'll give her a hand."

"That's okay. Kimberly and I can get it." Stephanie couldn't keep the urgency from her voice. She'd had a long, emotional day. The last thing she wanted was to be alone with him again. "There isn't much cleanup to paper plates and empty pizza boxes. You guys don't need to stay."

"Nonsense. I carried it in, I'll carry it out."

"Then I'm leaving." Leaning forward, Jennifer kissed her dad on the cheek then hugged Stephanie. "I'll call you tomorrow."

The rest of the group left as well, calling goodnights and thanking Brendan for the pizza.

In an unspoken routine, the remaining three each took on a task. Kimberly gathered glasses for the dishwasher; Brendan got a trash bag from the kitchen and made the rounds picking up the remains of the party. Stephanie gently lifted Max, now dosing into his shoulder, from his seat. Mindless of the cheesy sauce around his mouth and on the front of his shirt, she nestled him against her and carried him upstairs.

Taking a warm washcloth to his face and fingers, she wiped away the immediate remains of dinner before carefully undressing the sleeping child. Kissing him on the brow and laying him down on his toddler bed, she tucked the covers gently around her mini-Matthew. She heard the door to her daughter's room click shut. She'd enjoyed tonight. Kimberly missed the teasing and fun she'd had with Matthew. They both did. Tonight, for the first time since that last vacation, Kimberly seemed like her old self. For that much, Stephanie was thankful for Brendan's presence.

* * *

Brendan carried the trash to the bin out back then came into the kitchen. A wicker basket of assorted teas sat on the kitchen table. Perhaps a cup of tea would prolong the evening with Stephanie. The thought prompted him to fill the tea kettle and set it back on the stove to heat.

He noticed several things about her tonight that he thought had been lost from his memory bank. Her love for children was still very evident. She had often talked about wanting to be a mother. He also vaguely remembered her fear of not being able to have children. Now she had two. He could picture her as a little girl bringing home every stray on the block and he grinned at the thought. He'd been a stray of sorts. With no one lady in his life he'd gone from bed to bed. Yet he'd always come back to the one gentle hand.

He also remembered how organized she seemed. The first time she'd cleaned the house; he hadn't found anything without her help for weeks. Her cleaning spree had driven him crazy but also came to be one of the things he appreciated as well. She was capable of handling anything that came her way. The high school group tonight respected her.

She'd chosen the perfect place to raise her kids. A clean, wholesome town with strong moral values without restricting a child's growth, Eureka Springs emulated another time in history.

Kimberly, he thought with a bemused shake of his head. So much like her mother. She possessed Stephanie's passion for everything she did. The devotion to the Santa Club and to her baby brother amazed him for a girl her age. Most teenagers he had met cared only for themselves, bordering on rude. She, on the other hand, seemed polite and always willing to help.

There was something else about her, though he couldn't quite put his finger on it. Something seemed very familiar, yet he was sure he'd never seen her before; he'd not been around since Stephanie's wedding.

While waiting for the teakettle whistle, he searched for mugs and spoons. Selecting a soothing Chamomile for Steph and a spice blend for himself, he placed the tea bags in the cups and had just poured the water when she came in.

"Thought you'd like something to help you wind down." He handed her a mug. She had changed clothes. He surveyed slender legs in molded denim and admired the bulkiness of the sweatshirt. He'd bet his latest platinum album she wore nothing underneath. Confirming the wager, he detected a gentle sway as she leaned across the table for the honey crock. His hands itched to touch what he could only assume. Instead, he busied himself spooning sugar into his own tea.

"I hope Chamomile was okay?"

She nodded briefly before taking a tentative sip of the tea.

"Shall we sit out on the porch? It's a beautiful evening."

In reply she turned and went back down the hall. He followed, reaching past her just as they got to the screen door, pushing it open for her.

The warm, autumn breeze tousled her hair slightly, sending off a soft floral scent. Something stirred within him. A memory of snuggled warmth against an early morning chill with his face buried lightly in the back of her hair, rose to the surface. He shook his head at yet another part of his past he thought had drowned in the booze.

She settled into the white rocker, leaving him no other choice but the matching love seat. Love seats were for two people, not one. To combat the loneliness it evoked, he stretched across the seat, taking up as much room as possible. Drinking his tea, he watched her, waiting for her to say something, anything. Instead, she sat in silence, gazing off across the yard.

He knew he should be grateful she hadn't refused the tea or the request for him to sit a while. But the truth was he wanted more from her. Wasn't that a switch? There'd been a time when she had wanted more of him than he was ready to give. Why expect any different from her now? He needed to breach the silence, get her talking. He ventured on what he thought a safe topic to open the conversation.

"How'd you come by Whisker Dan?"

"Jennifer told me about him. He's done repair work at the hotel and often provides toys for children of holiday guests. The old guy's spent his entire life in these hills." She moved the rocker lazily back and forth. "Story has it his great great grandpa's the hand behind most of the cut work of this town. He keeps the repairs up on what is left."

She turned to point out something above the bay window and his heart skipped its rhythm. She looked so serene. Was it because she wasn't looking at him?

"See that header trim."

Brendan tore his gaze from her face to look at where she pointed. The porch light illuminated a carved design of a sun setting behind rolling hills, the tendril rays appearing to fold into themselves, tucking away another passing day.

"It's very beautiful,"

"Like every other bit of carving, latticework, and gingerbread trim around here. Most of it done by his ancestors and cared for by all the generations that followed."

He stood and leaned against a support post. Whether to hear her better or just be closer to her, he wasn't sure. He fought the impulse to touch her. A strong desire to apply hungry, demanding kisses to her full lips was almost too much for his self-control. To distract his hands, he took a stick of gum from his pocket and unwrapped it. Slowly he broke the gum into small pieces, putting them in his mouth one at a time.

"That's the kind of love I wanted these kids to feel on Christmas morning." Her voice reverberated with emotion. "We could have shopped for factory built toys like every other kid will get. But that's not what we saw."

"What do you mean?"

"Santa Club isn't just about giving dolls and trucks." Stephanie sat her cup on the small patio table then walked over to stand against the porch railing next to him. Her nearness drew him like a magnet. Gently he reached out, catching a strand of hair, twirling it around his finger. She made no attempt to break the contact, as her voice became almost a whisper.

"It's the memories, love, and hope. We want them to know if only for one day that they haven't been forgotten." She looked up at Brendan and he thought he'd melt in that moment. The conviction in her voice compelled him to take every word in, to make her cause his.

"Our hope is that as they get older, they'll remember a special Christmas morning in their life and share that joy with another child in some way."

Listening to her, he felt a tingle run the length of

his spine and an uneven beat to his heart. The woman truly was an angel. An angel he didn't deserve at this moment. But he would in time.

"Thanks for being here this evening. You don't know what your impromptu visit meant to Kimberly."

"What do you mean?"

"She misses Mathew. There are some things in her life I can't replace. On that window seat tonight, I caught a glimpse of the little girl in her."

"What about you Steph? What do you miss?"

"My children are my life. I'm glad you were here… for Kim's sake."

She rose on her toes to place a quick kiss on his cheek, letting a hand rest lightly against his chest only briefly before saying goodnight. Picking up their tea mugs, she went inside, closing the door behind her.

Brendan stood only moments before swinging off the porch by a post. He all but skipped down the sidewalk to his jeep, whistling into the night.

* * *

"And for mine," she whispered into the empty hall.

Stephanie leaned back against the closed door, realizing how it became increasingly difficult to not want him near. She had to bury that desire. Jennifer had said he was going to be working in Branson but she didn't say for how long. Soon Jennifer's wedding would be over and he'd be back on tour. Then what? She had Kimmie and Max to think of.

She couldn't trust her heart to him again. She held her breath, listening. Within moments, she heard the footfall of his boots on the sidewalk. The jeep roared to life and pulled away from the curb. Silence.

She exhaled slowly. He was gone. The awareness brought both relief and sorrow. Not since the first few weeks following Matthew's death had she struggled with the emptiness welling up within her now. Was it too much to want someone to hold her? The thought of not spending another night alone in the antique four-poster bed was tempting, yet his presence might have created other challenges.

Shaking the question from her mind, she carried the tea mugs into the kitchen and placed them in the dishwasher. Like a programmed robot, she added detergent, spot remover, and then clicked the door shut to start the routine evening process. Making a quick pass through the main floor, she turned out lights and locked doors before going upstairs.

After checking on the children, she went into her own room and closed the door only partway. Max had become adept at going anywhere in the house he pleased, but doorknobs still presented a challenge for the adventuresome toddler. Both children knew Mom's door was always open.

Going over to the bedside table, she opened a drawer and removed the small silver frame she kept there. The last year she and Brendan were together, his sister, Kris, had given her this picture of him. At the same time, Kris had taken a picture of Stephanie for a matching frame. She'd given it to him for his birthday that year. Did he still have that picture, or had it become lost in his travels?

Staring at the picture of the boyishly lean build and tousled hair of his youth, she saw a lot of Kimberly. Now he had a firmness and style achieved through time and maturity. It's no wonder women slept in ticket lines for front row seating at his concerts. The man was hot – plain and simple.

Slipping the frame back into the drawer, she eyed her reflection in the large cheval mirror in the corner. How did he see her? Did he see the same girl of twenty that told him to leave on that day? Or did he, too, notice changes. Changes in her that only time and the birth of children can bring.

Turning from the mirror, she took a nightgown from the bureau drawer and dressed for bed. With a touch of a button on the CD player Brendan's velvet voice floated from the speakers, wrapping her in its cocoon.

Snuggling beneath the quilt, she hugged the spare pillow to her chest. The impressionable softness didn't prevent the words of love from piercing her heart. Tears fell freely down her cheeks to the fluffy barrier she clutched. What she'd give to hear those words spoken only to her. Too many things prevented that from ever becoming a reality. One of them slept innocently in the bed across the hall.

CHAPTER 5

September drifted into October with very little change in the weather. The days were unseasonably warm and filled with activity. Gardner's had harvested the remains of their plantings and put the beds to rest for the winter. Quilts in a multitude of patterns and colors hung over porch railings and clotheslines. The sun would chase away the mustiness of storage, making them inviting for slumber. Such was the scene at Planned to Perfection.

Stephanie spent this Saturday morning preparing for the winter just as many of her neighbors. Bunches of Rosemary, Sage, and a variety of mints hung in the pantry. She enjoyed the tantalizing flavors the homegrown herbs gave to her cooking. Store bought seasonings paled in comparison.

Sitting on the porch drinking a cup of tea, she watched the couple next door switch the storm windows. She'd hated that job! Always managing to pinch her fingers more than once in the process, she'd tried to wait for Matthew to do them but her impatience to get things done often took over. That, and the more honey-do tasks she could accomplish left them with more family time when Matthew wasn't on duty. He'd intended to install replacement windows in their house in Indiana. The money never seemed to be available.

Replacement windows were one of the first upgrades she'd made to the cottage. Thankfully, there were ones available that fit within the strict city codes for historical preservation. Doing things on her own meant keeping tasks as simple as possible. Tasks like not having to change out the windows with the seasons.

So much for simplicity. Nothing had seemed simple since Brendan's reappearance in her life. Everything from putting Max down for a nap to the Art Club meeting last week had been complicated. One minute she would be doing things as always and the next, he'd appear and the bottom would drop out of her stomach. She prayed today would remain on an even track. She doubted he'd be around. He seemed to enjoy time off on the weekends.

Must be nice! She wasn't sure what an entertainer did when he wasn't performing. There had to be more to it than drifting around a tourist town twenty-four-seven. He enjoyed a lot more free time than she did. But then, he wasn't balancing a career and raising a family. He seemed to have pulled his life together, but his was on the road and hers was here. If he ever decided to stop touring, she knew he'd make a good father. But she also understood he had to make a living, just as she did with her company. Their worlds were as far apart now as ever.

The day was gorgeous. Cool evenings painted the leaves golden hues of yellow and orange. The warm autumn breeze made them dance to Mother Nature's Ozark tune. Days like this would become few and far between as winter drew near. Why was she chasing dust bunnies on a day like this? She'd finish up a couple of things then walk over to Becky's and pick up Max.

After finishing her chores, Kimberly always spent her spare moments with her best friend, Becky. She usually took her little brother along. The girls were great about watching him and Stephanie tried to balance it out for them. Kimberly helped at every opportunity. Most of the time she just seemed to whisk Max away without a word from Stephanie.

Maybe that was her way of keeping Matthew close. Stephanie had never really thought about it before. But then, she found herself dissecting a lot of things since Brendan's reappearance. She took her cup into the house as she thought about her son. He was getting so big. His third birthday was next month, and as he got older it became increasingly difficult for her to accomplish tasks without his 'help'. She'd have to see about a daycare or playgroup. As much as she'd like it to be so, he wouldn't stay Matthew's baby forever.

After completing a few minor tasks around the house, she put on clean clothes. She dressed in tan leggings, topped with a dark brown sweater, put on comfortable walking shoes. Slipping her cross-body bag into place, she went out the door and down the block.

Becky and her mom, Marge, lived in one of the many Victorian bungalows along Pine Street. A low white picket fence surrounded the yard. An open space where a gate once hung invited anyone to enter. Appropriately so for the cozy tearoom Marge operated from the rose colored cottage.

The girls were in the front yard, playing ball with Max when she arrived. He saw her instantly and ran out the gateway and down the sidewalk to meet her. Calls of "Mommy" wrapped her heart in a warm glow. Catching him up in her arms, their combined laughter rang into the clear autumn sky as she twirled him around.

"Mom, can I go to Bentonville with Becky and her Mom?" The girls joined them as she and Max approached the yard. "We want to do some shopping and maybe see a movie."

"I guess so, if it's okay with Marge."

"Yes!" Becky fist-pumped the air. "Can she spend the night?"

The girls were typical preteens. She remembered wanting to spend Saturdays at the mall with her best friend, watching boys and trying on clothes their parents would never have let them wear. It was part of growing up.

"Is your homework done?" Her mothering took over.

"All except a History test we're going to study for together."

"Sure," she smiled at her daughter. Leaving her

friends at such a difficult time in Kim's life hadn't been easy. Becky had taken her by the hand the first day of school and never let go. So much alike both in looks and personality, the girls might have passed for sisters. A cloud passed over Stephanie as she thought about a half-sister already in the picture.

"Moosic, moosic," Max yelled, chasing the cloud away.

"Okay, we'll walk downtown sweetie." He loved music and enjoyed listening to the traveling musicians in Basin Park.

"You girls have a good time."

"Thanks, Mom, we will," Kimberly hugged her and tousled Max's hair. "I'll be home in time for Sunday dinner."

Putting Max down to walk, Stephanie took his hand in hers. Mother and son made their way towards the heart of town.

An off-key guitar picker set the tone for ambling tourists. Brendan judged the man to be in his early sixties. It was hard to tell for sure. The man sported a wiry salt and peppered beard and shoulder length hair of the same color. Brendan knew the life well and that a man could become old fast if he wasn't careful.

Paying little attention to the tourists milling around the park, the musician moved from one soulful ballad to another. Only occasionally would he nod his head or touch the brim of the old felt hat he wore. All in thanks for tips dropped into the case at his feet.

Brendan sat on the steps outside the coffeehouse. As he listened, he thought back to his early days in the area. He'd been living in Branson for several months when Jennifer let him know she'd accepted a hotel manager's position here. He knew she'd looked for something in the area that would allow them more time together. Like him, she'd needed to get away and start fresh. After giving her some time to settle into her new job, he'd come down for a weekend visit and never left. The town and its people captured his heart. Coming here was like coming home. A feeling he'd never felt before in his life.

During those early days he spent the weekends in Branson. Three nights of theater production shows to packed auditoriums paid the bills. As soon as the curtain dropped on Sunday night, he'd hurry back to Eureka Springs.

Through the week he'd write and do what he loved most. This is where he played solely for himself and the peace it brought him. The park was a change from the lights, smoke, and tailgate traffic of the city. Here he felt the words he'd written, most of which became hits for him over the last few years. Every strain of emotion possible molded his musical style after dry out. Music was his therapy; the new lease on life. A life without Stephanie and the brain-fogging intoxicants.

But he was past the peddler stage. 'Brendan Keane' was a big name in the entertainment business now. He didn't have to spend his time sitting in a park on a warm fall day, playing old songs. People paid a lot to see him now. Nope, didn't need it at all. Yet, he found himself standing and stretching, he pulled his jeans legs down straight over his boots. Striding across to the transient, he dropped a few bills into the case.

"May I?" Brendan held out his hand.

The picker gave him a sparse-toothed grin as he shook Brendan's hand before relinquishing his lively hood. Bracing his right foot on the edge of the park bench and resting the guitar on his leg, he found the rhythm of an old folk tune.

With each strum of the strings, he felt the tension peel away like a second skin. As he went from folk to ballad and back again he relaxed, enjoying himself while fully aware of the amount of money being dropped in the musician's guitar case.

* * *

Stephanie stepped out of the bookstore with her son in tow. Shifting her bag to take his hand, a familiar ballad caught her attention, bringing a smile. She loved the weekends best. That's when most of the traveling musicians passed through town. She and Max had stopped in at the Grand Central Hotel earlier so he could 'play' the piano with the resident tickler. Somehow she didn't think the little guy'd had enough 'moosic'. He was now trying to pull her down the stone walk towards the park.

Smiling apologetically to people along the way, she followed him in the direction of the guitar strains. Reaching the steps of the coffeehouse, she froze. The day may be a typical fall Saturday but the scene before her was not.

The park had taken on a party atmosphere like

they usually only saw during Folk Festival weekend. Most everyone there was dancing, clapping, or singing along. And above the fiesta rose the most beautiful voice she had ever heard. The same voice that sang her to sleep every night.

"Bedan Mom! Bedan!" Max cried excitedly. She picked him up, settling him on a hip. His chubby hands clapped together in awkward time as he watched. When Brendan finished the song, everyone clapped and dropped money into the guitar case. Some handed him something to autograph or wanted their picture taken. Others were content to just shake his hand.

"Monies! Mommy, monies!" The boy kicked to get down. As the crowd was thinning, she saw no harm in handing her son some coins and putting him down. He loved to drop money into the case and talk to the musicians. She had little doubt her son would be a musician someday. In that respect he was more like Brendan than Matthew. Past listening to the radio, Matthew had no interest in music. Where their son got interest was beyond her.

She watched as he ran up to Brendan, pulling at his jeans. He looked down and she saw a questioning look cross his face as he scooped Max up. She smiled and waved at them. He said something to Max, pointing at her and the boy nodded. She felt more than heard Brendan's laugh; its melody reverberating off the buildings.

Stragglers made over her son. Brendan acted like the proud dad, brushing baby-fine hair out of the child's face or securing a snap on his jacket. Leaning against the wall, she became all too aware of the picture they made. Though the two shared no physical characteristics, they looked so right together. The thought both frightened and comforted her. One stone could crack the glass covering the picture they made and she held the biggest one of all.

Brendan, still carrying Max, walked over to where she stood. Her heart quickened as he approached. With the afternoon sun behind him, he appeared as a knight; his long legs striding with ease through the lingering crowd. A smile played across his face and she found it infectious. Max bounced and giggled with the rhythm of a jockey.

"Couldn't resist?" She nodded in the direction of the bench. The traveling musician was back in his spot. People continued to mill around, casting glances their way.

"It was my home for a long time. Part of the charm of this community is being able to do that. They all knew who I was but they let me have my moment."

"You sounded great." She never took her eyes from his. Fighting the impulse to close them against the vision before her, she moistened her lips with the tip of her tongue. The casualness of his stance pulled taut the watercolor western shirt he wore. His chest, squared and strong, threatened to pop the pearl snaps. Tightness filled her chest with the memory of the smooth skin beneath the material.

"Mommy, ice keam," Max said, reaching for her.

"The master has spoken it seems." Brendan laughed as he handed the little boy over. "My treat?"

"Ice keam!" he squealed, again.

She laughed. "Sure,"

Brendan relieved her of her shopping bag as she put her son down then the three

of them walked across the parkway to the ice cream shack.

Ordering a single scoop cone for Max and cola floats for themselves, the three sat on the steps leading to the curb. A comfortable silence settled in as they watched Max wear more of the melting chocolate confection than he ate. Occasionally, Stephanie wiped his mouth or fingers. Otherwise, she was unconcerned with the ice cream spatters to her son's jacket or the hand tracks on his jeans. These things were a given with children.

"Done." Max offered the remains of his cone to Brendan a few minutes later.

"Good job, buddy." Brendan took the cone and dropped it into his empty cup. "Now what shall we do?"

Playing with his shoelaces, Max appeared to give the question serious thought. The instant he made the decision as only a two-year-old was capable, his eyes began to sparkle and he grinned up at Brendan.

"Tolley!" his eyes danced. "Tolley, mommy," he sang, turning to her beseechingly.

Brendan looked at her over her son's head. She pretended not to notice as she pulled a towelette from her bag. With a mother's precision, she wiped away the worst of the chocolate from the cherub face and sticky fingers with just a couple of swipes.

"A trolley ride?" She grinned at her son and tapped him on the tip of his nose. "You just like to ring the bell."

There was no doubt her son had everyone wrapped around his chubby little finger. From his sister who would voluntarily give up her Saturday morning so Mom could get something done to the trolley driver who would let him ring the bell, he owned them all.

"Tolley mommy! Peas."

"Looks like we're taking a trolley ride." She turned to Brenda, who was already

standing. "Would you like to join us?"

Picking Max up and settling him in the crook of an arm, he extended his other hand to her. She eyed it only momentarily before accepting it with her free hand. A shiver coursed along her spine with the contact. She found herself unwilling to break the connection. He obviously felt the same as he laced his fingers with hers. Together the three of them made their way down the block to the trolley depot.

The depot was full of people. Several were pointing to locations on the large map, deciding on a colored route to take. A few stood in line at the ticket window. No one gave notice to the tall handsome cowboy with a toddler perched on his shoulders.

Looking around at the crowded open lobby, she was aware of the lack of attention paid to the superstar. She knew the way Brendan presented himself had a lot to with it.

There was no entourage following him everywhere, no limo waiting at the curb. He was just Jeep Cherokee Brendan. He didn't dress or carry himself as the highest paid entertainer in the business. To an unsuspecting person, he was just another dad spending the day with his son.

A warm glow welled up inside as she saw what everyone around them must see. It should be Matthew standing here waiting to take Max for a trolley ride. Yet even as she closed her eyes, it wasn't her late husband she envisioned. Eyes open or closed, Brendan still stood there.

"Here we go buddy," Brendan's voice interrupted the direction her thoughts had gone. Taking Max from his shoulders and putting him down, Brendan enveloped a small hand in his. Stepping aside, he motioned for her to board first. Knowing her son's passion for ringing the bell, she slid into the seat behind the driver. Brendan sat next to her, balancing Max on his left knee.

Heat radiated from Brendan. Near tangible flames licked at hers where their thighs met. The close proximity was nearly her undoing. He felt it too, she was sure. His eyes twinkled with amusement as he looked at her, daring her to move away.

"Have enough room?" His voice, quiet and smooth as silk, fanned the flame within her.

She refused to reveal more than her blushed complexion already confessed. Instead, she focused on people boarding.

"Yes. I'm fine. I can put him on my lap, if you'd like. That would give you a little more room."

"He's okay. Aren't you buddy?" He jostled his knee, sending the boy into a fit of giggles.

"Pull the chord, Little Man," the driver instructed.

"Bell! Bell!"

With a clang of the bell, the driver put the trolley into gear and they were on their way.

She had chosen the red trolley route. The five-mile historic loop would take them the scenic route up to the Crescent Hotel. On the turn around, the driver would make a stop a couple doors from her house on its way back to the depot. The entire trip would take about thirty minutes, getting Max back home in time for a quiet supper and bed. And with any luck, Brendan would choose to get out at the hotel.

The trip went by quickly. The trolley wound its way along the historic residential path, treating the passengers to views of stone cottages and quaint Victorians. Locals gathered in their quilts before the evening dew sat in. The smell of hamburgers grilling floated on the breeze.

Momentarily cloaked in memories of lazy Saturday afternoons, she turned to gaze out the window. Even before they'd married, Matthew had arranged to be off early on Saturdays. That was their afternoon. They'd gone on picnics, had cookouts with his friends from the department and taken walks in the early evenings.

All the things she had hoped someday to do with Brendan, Matthew had provided. She missed those days. Kimberly had been a part of those memories. What did she have to offer their son? Would he remember days like today?

She turned to look at Brendan. He'd been watching her. She'd felt it, just like always. Draping his free arm across the back of her seat, he gave her shoulder a reassuring squeeze. Instinctively she reached up, placing her hand over his. It felt right.

"Crescent!" The driver called as the trolley came to a stop at the entrance of the historic hotel.

She still held his hand as well as his gaze. Passengers disembarked yet neither of them moved.

"This is my stop."

She shared his reluctance to let go when he removed his hand from beneath hers.

"I've loafed long enough."

"Thank you for this afternoon Brendan." Realizing she truly meant it as she slid a dozing Max onto her lap.

"Can you get him home okay?"

"We'll be fine. Chet will stop right in front of the house for me."

"I'll bring your shopping bags down tomorrow. You can't carry both."

"Thanks. Join us for dinner? Dave and Jennifer usually spend Sundays with us."

"Last call for the Crescent Hotel."

"I'd like that. I'll see you then." Bending down, he brushed a gentle kiss to her lips before stepping off.

As the trolley pulled away, making the turn-around, she placed a free hand against the glass in a half-wave. The parting smile he shot her put another crack in the already crumbling wall around her heart.

* * *

Brendan watched the trolley descend the hill

away from the hotel. With a courteous nod to the doorman, he turned and went up to his suite. He checked his phone for messages. After returning calls, he sat on the couch, satisfied with how his day had gone. The impromptu concert in the park had begun a something he hadn't been aware of needing. Tension within him flowed away like the healing springs, replaced with a sense of contentment. Creativity he felt he'd lost somewhere along the way surfaced with the strumming of the guitar. A voice from within suggested he might be happier if he didn't go back on the road.

Then there was the feeling of pride as he'd held Max. Experience told him to protect the little guy from any paparazzi that might be in the crowd. Yet gut instinct led him to act like a father, being nonchalant about the attention and removing the boy from the situation as calmly and as quickly as possible. Last but certainly far from least, was Stephanie. He'd not missed the look of confusion flickering across her face as he'd held Max. What had she been thinking? She was a good mother. She'd trusted him with her son, turning Max lose to run to him. That small gesture spoke volumes in his book.

He also knew from conversations with Jennifer that there'd been no one special in

Stephanie's life since coming to Eureka Springs. He was further inclined to believe that relaxing days like today didn't fit her schedule often. That is where he intended to start. Stephanie Douglas was about to be reminded that life existed outside of the office. They would experience that life together.

CHAPTER 6

Stephanie flipped through the appointment book. Nearly every day for the next two months, except for Sundays, was full. It seemed as if the fall colors brought more weddings to Eureka Springs than any other time of year.

Her preference would be in the spring when the dogwoods bloomed profusely, creating one huge petal-soft cloud throughout the valley. The glow cast by a full moon filtering through the trees was perfect for a late evening stroll with that special someone.

Slamming the book closed in agitation; she tossed the pen onto the desk. What did she know about moonlight strolls and romance? Those had been fine, naive thoughts in the early days with Brendan.

They'd never taken a moonlight walk in their time together. Instead, they'd played in nature's spotlight as it shown across the island of his bed.

That was a time when she truly believed loving him would be enough. Growing up had been a hard step when she realized he had to return that love.

She and Matthew had shared a different type of love – one grown from mutual respect and friendship. Theirs hadn't been the flame-consuming passion she'd felt for Brendan. Yet, she would have given her life for his.

But he wasn't physically here. He couldn't hold her, touch her shoulder, brush a stray hair from her face, and kiss her... Stephanie put a hand to her lips with a moan. Those days were gone. He'd never touch her again. That didn't stop her body from wanting to experience those moments. Brendan would do them all so well.

A week had passed since their day with Max. Everything felt so right. The way he'd buddied up with the toddler or the quiet solace he'd conveyed when he knew she'd been thinking of Matthew.

The Sunday dinner went just as well. Dave and Jennifer were like family. Over the last year, they'd all found their special task. Jennifer brought a salad and a vegetable. Stephanie provided the potatoes and the meat, which Dave carved. Since her introduction to the kitchen, Kimberly usually made a dessert of some type.

To this particular dinner, Brendan arrived with the ingredients for a Green Bean casserole. He'd also brought a replenishing supply of assorted teas and flavored coffees in an antique Stafford shire footed bowl.

Just as they'd done the night of the art club meeting, everyone took on an unspoken task for after dinner clean up. From there, they'd spent the rest of the evening playing board games. Brendan was the first to leave, professing an early meeting in Branson the next day; but not before she'd let slip an open invitation. He was welcome anytime.

"What was I thinking?"

"I don't know. What were you thinking?" Kimberly came into the room and leaned on her mother's desk.

"That it's almost lunch time." She evaded the question that was sure to start a long conversation full of answers she wasn't ready to give. "Getting hungry?"

"More so than normal?"

"How about Cindy's? One of the turkey club's sound really good."

"Okay, but I'm not sharing with you," Kimberly admonished with a grin. "You can share with the munchkin." She motioned towards her brother who was intent on a movie.

The bell above the main entrance tingled. Darn it! Why hadn't she locked the door? She tried to remember on the weekends. The sign out front stated 'CLOSED SAT. & SUN.' But it didn't stop someone who just had to plan an event of some sort at the last minute. She stopped halfway to the door as Brendan stepped out of the hallway into the room.

"Bedan!" Max quickly lost interest in the movie. His chubby arms wrapping around one of Brendan's ever jean-clad legs.

Tightness formed in her chest as he picked the child up into a bear hug. They made a wonderful picture. Too wonderful, she thought, wishing more than ever that she'd locked the door.

"Brendan!" Kimberly spun away from the desk. "What are you doing here?"

"Hey, kiddo. I thought I'd see if anyone had a taste for a cinnamon roll."

"You must be psychic. We were just talking about going to Cindy's for lunch."

"So how 'bout it? Can I take the Douglas clan to lunch?"

"Mom, please."

Stephanie looked from the pleading look of her daughter to the boyish grin on Brendan. Instincts told her to decline, but remembering how he'd related to Kimberly she shook her head in resignation.

"I guess so. Will you please take Max upstairs and get him ready?"

"Cool! Come on squirt, let's get your coat on."

"Bedan do it," Max protested, clutching tighter to his friend's neck.

"Go ahead buddy." He disentangled the toddler's laced fingers from behind his neck. "I'll wait right here for you. Promise."

Stephanie watched as her son reluctantly went to his sister. As soon as she was sure the children were out of hearing she leveled her best 'I'm the mom, that's why' look at Brendan.

"Why do you do that?"

"What?"

"Just show up! You're everywhere I turn lately. I can't do anything with my children without you becoming a part of it."

"Ah, come off it Steph. It's lunch for cryin' out loud. What are you afraid of?" He spoke calmly, his gaze steady. "You look like you need to eat. You're smaller than I remember."

"I can't be smaller than I was thirteen years ago, I've had two kids." But she knew there was some truth to what he said. Since Matthew's death and raising the kids by herself, she didn't eat right. There always seemed to be something that needed done and by evening she was just too tired. She sighed, massaging her temples.

"That's better."

She wanted to slap the victorious smile off his face. He was just too sure he'd get his way.

Within a half-hour the four of them had taken the trolley down to the depot. From there, they'd gone to Basin park first so Max could listen to the "moosic". It allowed the heavy lunch rush to clear out of the tiny eatery. Kimberly took charge of her brother as they turned to leave the park. Soft as the flutter of butterfly wings, Stephanie sensed Brendan's hand at the small of her back. Together they crossed the street to the plank skywalk leading to the eatery.

Cindy's sat on the second floor of a collection of businesses built on the lower level. Another street ran along the upper level with stores on either side. The plank board skywalk was one way of connecting the two levels. Alternate routes were the narrow forked streets or a myriad of stairs peeking from between the tall middle row of old brick and stone buildings. Thus giving Eureka Springs the nickname, 'stair-step town.'

Brendan held the wooden screen door open for them. As usual, the place was busy. Several ice cream parlor tables were scattered to one side of the small room. An ice cream bin and a condiment bar took most of the other side. The line started at the opposite end of the room.

A family run business, one of the older children stood behind the register taking customer orders. A younger sibling took a cinnamon roll from the pan and put it on a paper plate. By customer choice, the made-from-scratch confection was drizzled in rich, snow-white icing or left plain. A plexi-glass wall allowed visitors to the café to see batches of cinnamon rolls in progress and waiting their turn in the oven.

The proprietor bantered with his family and customers as he created a fresh batch of the sweet rolls. A pleasant woman came in and out of the kitchen as if caught in a revolving door. She'd put a plate laden with a sub sandwich large enough for two and a generous amount of chips on a tray at the counter. Each order was served with a "hello" and a sincere smile.

Stephanie led the way to a vacant table.

"If you want to hold the table, I'll stand in line." Brendan took the booster seat Kimberly had secured and settled Max in. "What would you like?"

"I'll have a turkey club."

"Me too," Kimberly added to which Max piped "Me!"

"We'll share." Stephanie playfully tapped her son's nose. "He'll eat mostly chips anyway."

Through lunch she listened to Brendan and

Kimberly. He seemed to show a genuine interest in her likes and dislikes. Her daughter bubbled as she talked about school, her friends, and things she enjoyed.

"Mom, can I take Max to Becky's," Kimberly asked as they finished eating.

"I guess. You really don't have to take him. Why don't you and Becky enjoy yourselves?"

"That's okay, we like the squirt," she said, grinning. "He's fun. Besides, he'll be ready for a nap soon."

"All right. Here are the trolley passes."

They sat, neither speaking, for a few moments after the children had gone. Other than the night after the club meeting, they'd never really been alone. She knew what they should talk about but she wasn't ready to go there. Not yet. Brendan broke the silence.

"I'm going to get a refill. Want one?" He picked up his glass and motioned to hers.

"No, I'm fine, thanks."

"I'll be right back."

She watched as he unfolded his long legs from beneath the small table. With grace and assurance, he strode across the deli to the soda fountain. No one stopped him and that still amazed her. She wondered how someone in his position moved around so freely. He seemed to draw less attention now as an entertainer than he had when they were together before. Then he'd had the attention of every girl from fourteen to forty-plus. Any kid too drunk or embarrassed to face their parents knew Brendan's couch was always available - no questions asked.

"You're deep in thought." Brendan resumed his place at the table.

"I just can't get over how you move around so undisturbed." She shook her head in bewilderment. "You are a top draw on the concert circuit, yet you walk around this town untouched. It's like you're invisible or something."

"What I am isn't important. When I'm not performing I'm just Brendan Keane. I'm someone's son, someone's father."

She winced inwardly at the last word, watching as he took another long draw from his soda. Slowly, yet without hesitation, she reached across the table to rest her hand on his forearm. Her gaze never left his.

"Someone's first love."

Sitting the glass down, he reached for her hand. With slow precision, he traced the length of each finger with his own. A low growl escaped his lips as he turned the palm of her hand up and kissed it tenderly before clasping it between both of his.

"You tempt me so Stephanie. I know what I want, Angel. But you're not sure yet. That's okay. I can wait. Lord knows I've gotten good at it."

Slowly she pulled her hand free, unwilling to break the contact. She knew about steps and she wasn't prepared to take the first one on the journey that lay before her... for all of them. It was very warm all of a sudden. She had to get some air.

"Shall we walk?"

"Sure." He pushed back his chair, reaching over as he did so to pull hers out as well.

Hand in hand they walked along Spring Street looking in shop windows. As they shared opinions on the various handcrafted items, jewelry, and quilts she allowed herself to just enjoy the day.

On the way back to the trolley they paused at Sweet Spring. Brendan sprawled across the park bench while she chose to stand overlooking the spring. The melodic tune of the waterfall washed through her.

Why couldn't it always be like this? The day had turned into an enjoyable "family" day but she knew it wouldn't last. Once Jennifer's wedding was over he'd be gone. How was she going to prepare the kids? They were both growing quite attached to the singing playboy.

At home later as she reflected on the afternoon, a tornado began to churn within her. Common sense told her to put a halt to these outings. End things before Max began to see Brendan as a father figure. Kimberly would be hurt but she'd rebound. Yet Stephanie's heart ruled every time she looked into those chocolate brown eyes or felt his touch. The man cast a spell she didn't want to break.

* * *

"It was incredible Jen. I've never experienced anything like it."

Brendan paced his daughter's office as she finished up for the day. The day with Stephanie and the kids had gone as he'd planned. All except for a feeling he'd experienced while waiting in line to order their lunch.

"This… this glow seemed to settle around the three of them. The hairs on my neck bristled."

"Well you know I couldn't work in the Crescent without some belief in ghosts." His daughter eyed him quizzically. "What do you think it was?"

"Not what honey, who?"

"You mean Matthew?"

He stopped pacing, bracing his large hands on the desk. "Yes."

"There might be validity to what you saw. How do you feel about him keeping an eye on things?" Jennifer slid the ledger into a drawer then closed the coordinating program on the computer

"I don't know. I'm not even sure I believe it was… Matthew." He resumed pacing. "But if it was, I'll prove to him that his family is in good hands."

"You really love her don't you?"

Brendan all but dropped into the chair across from his daughter. Knowing it inside was one thing. But to voice it was an entirely different feeling. The admission came out soft and reverent.

"I do. God help me Jennifer, but I do. And it isn't just Stephanie." His voice lifted excitedly. "It's the whole family thing. This is my chance to truly be a husband and…" his voice trailed. How could he say what he felt without hurting his own daughter?

"And father?" Jennifer got up from her chair and came around the desk to kneel beside him.

He turned, enveloping his daughter in a hug. He'd missed out on so much of her life. By rights, she should near despise him for not being there; for wanting to be a father to someone else's children but she wasn't. She was charitable, forgiving, and honest. In that respect Jennifer was a lot like Stephanie. The same characteristics he counted on to make it possible for them to be a family.

In his room later he cruised the TV channels. Regardless of where he stopped, the same picture came to his mind. Stephanie had looked ravishing standing at the spring earlier. The soft autumn breeze played with the hem of her lawn dress. What he'd felt then overtook him now as he replayed the vision. He'd had the strongest desire to pull her into his arms, to capture the scent of her as it wafted with the breeze. He'd wanted to hold her close, assure her everything would be fine between them if she'd only let him in.

With a groan, Brendan turned off the television and tossed the remote carelessly onto the coffee table. "It's a good thing cold water isn't in short supply," he thought as he headed for the shower.

* * *

"Want Bedan," Max stuttered through a hiccup. The tears began at the mention of bedtime over an hour earlier. Stephanie cuddled her son close to the soft terry robe that had replaced her soaked dress. A warm bath usually lulled him to a doze.

Tonight, however, the terrible two's struck with a vengeance and she'd worn most of what she'd irritably termed Hurricane Max.

"Mommy?"

"What sweetheart?" She stroked his soft chestnut

curls. Smiling, she thought how closely the color of her son's hair resembled Brendan's eyes... and Kimberly's.

"Bedan come here?"

"Not tonight baby. Maybe tomorrow." An idea flashed through her mind. "Hey, how about if you snuggle under your special quilt and I get you a surprise?"

"Spize?" The boy looked up at her wearily.

"I'll get Kimmie's MP3 player and you can lie here and listen to Brendan sing. How about that?" She crossed her fingers behind his back.

It seemed an eternity passed before the boy pushed to get down. He padded across the braided rug in footed pj's and climbed across the footboard of his toddler bed. Sliding beneath the bottom of the quilt, he tunneled like a mole until he'd reached his pillow at the other end. He was asleep by the time she had returned with the player. Her bear cub turned angel had fallen asleep.

She stood in the doorway of his room for a moment, watching him sleep. Fear tugged at her heart. Tonight had been a small display of what she might expect when Brendan left. She'd not be able to soothe him with the possibility of future visits. In just a few short weeks Brendan would be gone and she'd be the one picking up the pieces... again

CHAPTER 7

"Mom, how long does this need to be?" Kimberly and Becky sat at the dining room table wiring brightly colored autumn leaves into lengths of garland.

The third week of October was already upon them. With Halloween just around the corner, it was time to welcome fall in full force. Once the crisp morning air warned of cooler evenings, Stephanie began creating a warm, inviting refuge from the outer elements. The rose and mahogany tones were now accompanied by deep earth colors of gold, burnt orange, and brown.

"They need to go around the doorways into the office and the dining room." She clipped the artificial leaves from their stems into a pile for the girls to work from. "As soon as I've got this done, I'm going to work on the arrangement for the hall table and my desk. When you need a break, there's juice in the fridge."

"Okay, Mom. Are we going out for supper?"

"No, there's a roast in the oven."

Normally, she would make use of the ever-efficient crock pot but there was something about the smell of a roast slow-cooking in the oven that provided a sense of warmth and comfort to her home. She became her true self in the autumn, secure in who she was and what she wanted from her life. Some people felt a renewal of the soul in spring. For Stephanie, she found her balance at this time of year. With Brendan around, she needed all of the balance she could attract.

"Jennifer said she'd do a loaf of bread and bring it when she brings Max."

As if on cue, she heard a car door being shut, then another open and close.

"That must be them now. Keep wiring, I'll be right back."

"Someone order pumpkins and corn stalks?" Brendan grinned from behind a large orange pumpkin.

Stephanie felt the energy around her shift off-kilter as she stepped aside and held the screen door open for him to enter.

"How did you know?" How did he seem to know when she needed anything? That was the security she remembered. Although he'd not always been around, he'd shown up when she really needed him. Mostly when Dad was in one of his moods. It was comforting to know she didn't need him quite the same way now. Still, a feeling of warmth and safety felt like a cloak whenever he was around.

"I saw Jennifer with Max at the hotel and she

filled me in. I thought you could use some help."

"Well, actually, yes. The girls are making garlands for around the doors. I don't want either of them on the ladder."

"Are you still afraid of heights?" He placed the pumpkin on the hall table.

"Still." She playfully pushed him towards the dining room. Apparently the booze hadn't robbed him of all their time together?

She'd been changing a bulb over the bar one night when she'd taken a nasty tumble. From that moment on, the thought of climbing on something higher than a four-legged foot stool made her nervous. There were times when she had to use the small painter's ladder. She didn't like to, but being an independent business owner called for drastic measures sometimes. She did what she had to do to keep things running.

"The girls are in the dining room. Want a glass of tea?"

"Sure. I'll see if I can give them a hand."

She started down the hall, passing the doorway he'd just gone through. A smile crept into place as she heard her daughter squeal with delight. A sound she knew without even looking included a hug.

Kimberly accepted him as part of their family. Even Max, in a toddler way, welcomed him. She hoped it didn't all come crashing down around them. It was only a matter of time before the entertainer in him took over and he'd be back on the road. The husband and father she'd always hoped for didn't exist in Brendan.

The afternoon progressed amidst the rustling of

leaves and laughter. Brendan helped the girls, while she created table arrangements and a couple of herb wreaths. They were just balling up the last of the newspapers covering the table when Jennifer and Max came in. Stephanie squatted down for a hug. The child's eyes shone bright as stars, wrenching at her heart as he passed her by, running straight for Brendan.

"Bedan, me up."

Brendan laughed, picking him up for their head to doorframe game. A deep laughter and child giggles wafted after her as she and Jennifer went to put the final touches to supper.

Over dinner, the conversation turned to the wedding. With only six weeks left, a lot still needed to be done. She assured an anxious Jennifer that everything was right on schedule.

"How's the remodeling on the house coming?" Stephanie passed the butter dish to Jennifer.

"Slow." Jennifer buttered a slice of the still-warm homemade bread. "Dave has been so busy on the Silver Dollar City renovation project. They're putting in six-day weeks."

"Anything I can do at the house? I do know how to use a hammer. I may play a mean drum or guitar but I still have construction skills, you know, in case this music thing doesn't pan out."

His eyes sparkled with humor as he popped a piece of roast beef into his mouth. Aside from being a foreman on a construction crew, Brendan had remodeled the three room house on the hill overlooking the river into an efficient tiny house before anyone even knew what they were. Back then, Stephanie had sat and kept him company, held the ladder when necessary, provided lunch she had brought from the bar and replenished the beer from his cooler. Stephanie had been in awe of his skills and fell in love with what she'd thought would be their home as she watched the progress. She wondered what had become of their love-shack.

"No Dad, but thanks. Once the project is completed, he'll have more time."

"Miss Elaine called today." Stephanie attempted to distract her thoughts as she cut a piece of meat for Max. "Your dress is ready for a fitting."

"Great! You'll go with me, won't you?"

"I'd love to. Shall I call and set a time?"

"Sure. Whatever fits your schedule will work for me."

"Stephanie, I'm going to have to starve myself for a month before the spring tour." Brendan pushed his plate aside and leaning back in the ladder-back chair.

"Mom's the best cook! Wait until you taste her peach crisp. It's heaven." Kimberly closed her eyes dramatically and licked her lips.

"I have." He winked at Stephanie with a devilish grin. She felt herself blush, and watched his grin widen, knowing his comment had hit the mark.

"So Dad, did you get the pumpkins?" Jennifer pushed her own plate aside.

"Yep. We can't do fall decorating without carving jack-o'-lantern." He tousled Max's hair where he sat in the booster chair next to him. "Steph, I found a long one I thought laid on its side would make a good base for an arrangement for the table. I meant to bring it in earlier. Kimberly, why don't you and Becky get the pumpkins out of the back of the jeep? He stood as he spoke, retrieving his keys from his pocket.

Stephanie's gaze became riveted to the sight before her. The room appeared smaller as she watched him slide his fingers deep into the front pocket of his wranglers. She moistened her suddenly too-dry lips with the tip of her tongue.

"Come on Steph, we'll get the table cleaned off." Jennifer stood and began gathering the dishes.

Stephanie blindly stacked the plates in the immediate vicinity as she continued to watch Brendan's movements. The black T-shirt appeared too small for his build as he lifted Max from the booster seat. A rush of desire swirled like a whirlpool as she imagined her fingers sliding across his shoulders, feeling each ripple of muscle beneath the fabric.

"Did you bring newspapers from the hotel for me?"

"Yeah, Dad. There's a bundle on the back seat of my car."

"Come on buddy. If I have to work, so do you."

"Me." Max was way ahead of him on the run to the front door.

"Looks like you and Dad are getting along pretty well."

Jennifer rinsed the dishes and put them in the dishwasher as Stephanie wrapped the leftovers and put them away.

"We're doing okay."

"Think you two will get back together?"

Stephanie closed the refrigerator and leaned against it, cross folding her arms. How did she answer that? There had been times over the last few days when she'd asked herself the same question. She'd already come to the conclusion she still loved him. But that didn't mean they were compatible. After all, she'd learned the hard way that love wasn't enough.

"There are too many facets to this relationship. It's hard to know. There always seems to be something blocking our path. Last time it was your dad's drinking; now it's his job. He's away from home for months at a time. That's not exactly stability. Not for kids, anyway."

"You haven't told him about Kimberly, have you?"

The question struck her like lightning. As if in a trance, she watched Jennifer take a wallet from her purse. Flipping to the pictures, she handed it to Stephanie.

With trembling fingers, she reached for the wallet. Two pairs of chestnut eyes stared back. With only the telltale differences depicting one picture to be older than the other, they might have been of the same smiling two-year-old. With the whisper of a touch, she ran one finger across the face of each picture, Jennifer's on the left and Kimberley's on the right.

Slowly, she closed the wallet and handed it back. The unspoken questions floated on the stillness of the room.

"Wh … Where did you get that picture?"

"Kimberly took a baby picture to school for a

project a couple of weeks ago. She came by the hotel on her way home. I found it on the floor of my office after she'd gone. It must have fallen out of a book." Jennifer snapped the wallet closed and returned it to her purse. "When I first saw the picture, I thought it was of me but couldn't imagine how it got there. Then I saw her name on the back."

"How.... I mean, why didn't you say something?"

"I figured you'd tell me when you were ready. Does she know?"

Stephanie shook her head. Her daughter grew up knowing one father. Matthew. How would she react to this? Stephanie gave a lot of thought to how Brendan would take the news. She'd never thought of what it would do to Kimberly.

"Your dad doesn't know, does he?" She felt more than heard the panic rising in her voice.

"No, I don't think so. At least, he's not said anything."

"He has to hear it from me Jen, I just don't know..."

"Come on gals, the pumpkins await," Brendan strolled into the kitchen. He stopped in his tracks. "What's wrong?"

" Noth...nothing." Stephanie took a napkin from the holder and turned away. She wiped at her eyes, trying to compose herself.

"Just a difficult time of year for me."

She stood and began gathering spoons and the special pumpkin carving knives from the utility drawer. She couldn't look at him. Not until she was sure he would not read the volume of information swimming in her eyes. She inhaled, then exhaled slowly as she turned back to Jennifer and Brendan.

"We need to get moving on the pumpkins. Max won't last much longer."

In no time, six grinning jack - o- lanterns lined the window seat. Halloween was still a couple weeks off, yet the conversation turned to costumes as cleanup began.

"Costumes. Oh shoot! I knew I'd forgotten something."

"What! What!" Kimberly and Becky cried in excited unison.

"Following the Halloween party at the hotel for the teenagers, there's to be a costume ball." Jennifer pressed her hands together, eyes twinkling. Stephanie already didn't like where this was headed.

"Way cool! What are you going as Mom?"

"Me? Oh heavens, I won't even go. This will be your first party." She smiled at her daughter, reaching out to cup her chin. "I'd rather be home to hear about your night."

"Ah, Mom, you gotta go. You don't have any fun. Brendan could be your date."

"Kimberly!"

"Just what I was thinking, Kim."

He bowed low before Stephanie. "It would be an honor dear lady. Would you accompany me to the ball?"

A tangible silence hung over the room as all eyes zeroed on her. Biting at her bottom lip, she looked from one expectant grin to another. A full evening with Brendan? As a date? Just the thought gave her goose bumps. This would be their first ever official date. Besides, they might even have fun. And costumes, carefully chosen, would afford him further privacy from fan attention. What could be the harm?

In response to his theatrics, she offered her hand with a curtsy.

"I would be delighted, sire."

They stood transfixed by one another as cheers roared around them. Stephanie knew she'd crossed a bridge. She was moving forward.

Later, when the house had quieted down, Brendan bagged the remains of the pumpkin carving while Stephanie put water on for tea. The girls took Max up to get him ready for bed. With a hug to Stephanie and her father, Jennifer went back to her cottage near the hotel. By the time the tea was ready, he had a fire in the fireplace.

"I hope you don't mind?"

"No, not at all." She handed him one of the mugs of tea. The room was very relaxing, despite his presence. Or maybe because of it.

"With the dampness from the coming storm, a fire sounded inviting."

His head rested on a pillow he'd placed on the back of the couch and he stretched his long legs out from the reclining position. He had taken his boots off at some point and now wiggled his toes in the confines of the wool socks. The man was sexy any way you looked at him.

"Comfortable?"

She sat facing him, tucking one leg beneath her. Bracing her head on the back of the couch with her left hand, she watched him. This moment might have happened thirteen years ago. Cans of beer would have replaced the mugs of herbal tea and his eyes would have been closed from intoxication. Now he breathed softly in total relaxation.

Her fingers shook as she reached to comb the tips of her fingers through the hair at his temples; so soft and fine. Using her thumb, she applied the slightest of pressure just above his ear in a circular motion.

"Mmmm, feels good," he whispered, his eyes still closed. "Didn't you used to do that?"

"Yeah. I didn't know if you'd been aware of it."

He opened his eyes and looked at her.

"I might not have been then. Now a touch or a smell can trigger something familiar."

"What led you to recovery? I mean, alcohol was your life for a very long time."

Brendan sat up, pulling his legs to a sitting position. Cupping the mug in both hands, he stared into the amber liquid. At first, she wasn't sure he was going to answer. So much so, that his voice startled her when he finally spoke.

"Several incidents brought me here. I guess there was a needling the day you told me we were finished. Next to the booze, you were the only constant in my life."

"That's why I did it Brendan. 'Next to me' is the key phrase there. The drinking always came first. Maybe you thought I was selfish to want to be number one in your life."

"No, not at all," Brendan turned to face her. She felt it as his new way of dealing with life. To deal with things head on. She waited for him to continue.

"You should have been in first place all along.

Lord knows you deserved it. I just didn't see it at the time. I think the drinking got worse after that. About three months after you closed the door on me, I blacked out. While I was driving, I think"

"Oh Brendan."

Did she really want to hear this?

"Were you hurt?"

"Not physically. I'm not even sure where I'd been or where I was going. I remember leaving work around noon. The next thing I knew, I was in a jail cell in the next county."

His hand shook, splashing tea over the rim of the cup. He sat the cup on the end table. Brushing his hand on his jeans as he stood, Brendan walked over to the fireplace. She watched him rub the back of his neck in an attempt to release the tension she knew knotted there. She'd experienced the same when he'd asked about Matthew.

He stuffed his hands into his front pockets, his head down, watching the flames. She knew that somewhere in that moment, he was somewhere else.

"I sat in that cell for a month. I couldn't bail myself out, wasn't even sure I wanted to. The first few days were hell. I wanted a beer so bad I cried like a baby for his bottle. They took my driver's license and shipped me off to rehab. In that three months of counseling and group therapy I realized I was an alcoholic, fighting the battle between needing a drink and wanting a life. The best thing was I discovered I could play the drums and the guitar… sober."

"And the road to stardom began." Stephanie got up and crossed the room to where he stood. She looked into his face, searching for any part of the old Brendan left. She needed to know for sure that man no longer existed.

"Well, not quite that easily." He took her hand. In an unspoken invitation, they settled onto the hooked rug in front of the fireplace. "Recovery is a life of ups and downs. One minute, the world can be perfect and the next..." Brendan snapped his fingers; "...you're right back down again. Thankfully, I only hit hard bottom once after treatment."

"What caused it? I mean, I know enough about the program to know alcohol addiction has a trigger like any other emotion."

"Right. My trigger was your wedding day."

Silence descended upon the room like the calm before a storm. She wasn't sure what to say or how to react.

"About a week after being released, I started wading through the house. Not only did I have to face things I couldn't remember but also there was everything that had accumulated while I'd been in treatment. Your wedding invitation for one."

"Oh Brendan."

"Yeah. I'd thought of you a lot through the process. I'd already made the decision to put my life together -finally. Then I was coming after you. I don't know what made me think you'd have ditched Matthew for me. But it was a nice dream."

His shrug spoke volumes. She knew in that instant, when his dream shattered, they were through. She thought back to all the times they'd been together. She'd been the one to replenish his empty beer, like a faithful servant. Had she been an enabler, part of his problem? Stephanie didn't want to think so.

"A dream shattered by an engraved invitation. Brendan, I'm so sorry." She reached out, placing a hand on his thigh.

"At the time, beer sounded really good. What did I have to be sober for? You were all I wanted and that was over. Or would be in a few hours. I found the invitation on your wedding day."

"Did you…"

"Did I get drunk? No. I went to the church. Stood in the back of the room and realized I wanted what you had. Even if I couldn't have it with you. You looked so happy, and I was happy for you. You said 'I do' and I realized I did too. I walked out of the church in search of a way to exorcise you from my heart and find my own happy."

"Did it work?"

"Have you listened to my music?" He laced his fingers with hers. "I thought by getting my thoughts on paper, the heartache into the music would be a cleansing of sorts so that I could start over. You see where it led me."

"I didn't know." She couldn't stop the tremble in her voice or the tears falling down her cheeks. She didn't even bother to swipe at them. Instead, she saw them reflected in his eyes and knew he felt them, too. "If I had thought we stood a chance, I'd have waited. I just didn't see it. Three years was long enough."

Brendan lifted his hand to her cheek, brushing a tear aside with his thumb. Gently, he leaned forward, catching the next ones with the tip of his tongue. She moaned. Never in her wildest dreams had she ever imagined being with him like this again. As his arms gathered her close, she eagerly accepted the sensations his nearness offered.

Every inch of skin along her collar bone and throat sizzled where his tongue trailed. When he kissed her, she drank thirstily, matching each probe with her own. As a teenager, she'd relished in the things they had done. Neither those nor any of her time with Matthew had prepared her for what she felt now.

Warning bells sounded in her subconscious. What was she doing? What was it about this man that drove every sensible thought from her mind with a kiss or a touch? She refused to allow herself to make the same mistakes. Pushing the palms of her hands against his chest, she strove for coherency.

"Brendan, stop. Please. We.... I can't do this. Not yet."

"Angel, what's wrong?"

The look of honest concern in his eyes calmed her. She knew instinctively that even if he didn't love her, Brendan had never stopped caring.

"This just isn't right. I want you so bad it hurts. But I have responsibilities. If I learned one thing in our time together before, actions have outcomes. I'm not sure either of us is ready for the direction we were going."

She watched as he turned away to stare into the glowing remains of the fire. Then he stood, hauling her up with him. Butterflies fluttered around her heart when he looked into her eyes. There was a sobered gentleness she'd always craved.

"You always were the one with the control. Be glad I'm a gentleman. Besides, I told you once that when we made love, you'd better be able to swim." His gaze traveled from the collar of her T-shirt to the tips of her moccasins. "And frankly, Angel, you're a bit overdressed."

With a quick kiss to her lips, he tugged on his boots and was gone. She stood, staring after him only moments before laughing softly with a shake of her head. The man was wonderful.

* * *

"Hi, Patricia. Do you mind if I use the piano for a bit?"

"Of course not, Mr. Keane. Go right ahead. I'll get you some coffee," the desk clerk offered.

"I'd prefer herbal tea if you have some."

"I'll bring it right over."

Shaking his head, Brendan walked across the lobby to the piano. His late night composing sessions were usually done with a strong decaf coffee. Recently, though, he drank herbal tea. Was that even a guy's drink? The road crew would rib him for his new choice in libation, he was sure. He wanted to prove to Stephanie he'd changed, but he hadn't counted on herbal tea being a part of the transformation.

After leaving her house, his emotions were running too high to go back to his solitary room. Personal emotions were the basis for his biggest hits. As the creative juices flowed, he had driven downtown to the Grand. A beautifully old piano graced the lobby of the period hotel. Walking through its doors was like entering a time warp. It was easy to envision men in tails and top hats. Ladies in bustles and plumed hats would be on their arm, nodding a greeting to other quests.

Now, he sat at the piano. Almost of their own volition, his fingers found the chords that matched his mood. A soft, tender melody swirled around him as he came to terms with the depth of his love for Stephanie. The tempo increased, pulsing with the intense frustration of unfulfilled passion.

He knew she loved him. She had to. Why else would she agree to the date or kiss him as if trying to swallow him whole? She was passionate about the things she believed in. The depth of those feelings was very evident this evening. She was on the brink of surrender. He felt it. But something was holding her back.

He felt the invisible wall come between them each time he ventured close. Was it Matthew? The vision in the café still haunted him. Was it her love for the man who had fathered her children?

The new melody he'd been working on at the piano still swirled in his head as he drove back to the Crescent over an hour later. Lyrics came and went as he further pondered the barrier between them. How could he convince Matthew that he'd care for the kids as if they were his own? The man was dead! And how was he supposed to convince Stephanie that he'd changed if she kept halting his advances? If he could figure out what was holding her back then he'd know his next move.

She'd agreed to the costume ball. That was a start. As he parked the jeep and went up to the room, his mind reeled with ideas. Stopping at the top of the stairs, he grinned. He would make the most of the evening. It was his one chance to be truly alone with her. By the end of the night, his angel would have no choice but to admit her true feelings. From there it would only be a matter of time. Tossing his keys into the air and catching

CHAPTER 8

Stephanie stared at her reflection in the mirror. What she saw surprised her. The woman looking back appeared thinner than she remembered. The eyes that once sparkled with life now seemed dull and forlorn. Where had the bright-eyed wife and mother gone?

Agitatedly she adjusted the ornate Spanish comb for what seemed the hundredth time. A mass of cascading curls created by a local beautician fought the restraint. Struggling with a wayward strand, she pondered her own question. The wife had died with Matthew and the mother just too tired to care most days. The businesswoman filled up most of the time card.

By the end of the workday motherly duties waited on the side. Once dinner, baths, homework, reading, and school functions took over nothing of the day remained. A quick shower, a cup of tea, and a pillow completed the last round of the clock.

Tossing the comb onto the dressing table in frustration, she buried her face in her hands. What was she thinking? She couldn't go through with this. Being alone with Brendan wasn't safe. She'd never been able to resist his devilish charm. She had almost given herself to him the other night. Being in his arms tonight would be asking for trouble. Maybe she should claim ill and crawl into bed, away from everything.

"No! Jennifer's right, I do need more time to myself." And tonight is a good place to start. She'd dance and enjoy being with him again. That would be easy. Keeping it from going beyond the party would be the real challenge.

She still wanted him physically and if their recent encounter was any indication, the feeling was mutual. She'd been the voice of reason then and she would be tonight. She had to be. This evening could not go any farther than the masquerade ball. Her life existed here in Eureka Springs with Kimberly and Max. His life was wherever his tour manager sent him. On a daily basis, the tabloid headlines spouted broken marriages and affairs in an entertainer's life. It came with the territory. That's not the life she wanted for her family. Tonight they would be the proverbial ships passing in the night.

She sighed as a tap sounded at the door, followed by Jennifer's voice.

"Steph, may I come in?"

"It's open." Stephanie got up from the dressing table and walked over to stand before the cheval mirror.

"I found this choker at a …wow!"

Jennifer froze just inside the door. Stephanie couldn't help but laugh at the look of astonishment on Snow White's face behind her reflected in the mirror.

"Well?" Stephanie twirled in place. The layers of tulle beneath the wide, black satin skirt rustled with the sway.

"It's terrific. You are going to be the belle of the ball."

"I don't know why I agreed to this." She muttered pulled the cap sleeves farther up onto the top of her shoulders. The gesture caused the bodice to dip lower. She tugged furtively at the lace overlaid satin material in hopes of covering the swell determined to escape the confines.

"I feel like I'm going to my first prom."

Jennifer stepped behind her to fasten a black velvet choker into place. Stephanie adjusted it to center the cameo as her friend slid the sleeves back off the shoulder with a wicked grin.

"You made it through that one okay, didn't you?"

"This is my first."

Stephanie had moved to Fulton Hill, Indiana in the middle of the school year. Cliques had already formed and she was an outsider from the beginning. No friends meant no dates. Instead, she'd gotten a job waitressing in a local bar where she'd met Brendan just before Christmas. She found it interesting that the town she had left behind two years ago included a statue of Christ of the Ohio while her forever home now included the Christ of the Ozarks. Was her life coming full circle?

She turned to face Brendan's daughter. With the short cut, raven black wig, Jennifer looked more like him than ever. Who could have thought that little girl in pigtails would become her best friend? Then, she had envisioned Jennifer as a stepdaughter. Was that still a possibility? Not likely. Their lives were still worlds apart.

"Well, your date is meeting you there. Dad's into the whole mystique of this." Jennifer laughed. "He says you have to 'find him'."

"Oh great. As if I'm not nervous enough, your dad wants to play hide and seek."

"It'll be fun. Besides, you look incredible. I only hope Dad doesn't play his game too long. Every man in that room will be vying for your attention, Senora."

Stephanie took a last look at the reflection of the Spanish maiden costume she'd found at a costume shop earlier in the week. No one had ever heard of a golden-haired senora but something about the costume left amongst the meager selection had spoken to her.

"I doubt that, but thank you anyway. Speaking of kids games, did you have any trouble with Max?"

Jennifer had volunteered to drop Max off at Marge's when she and Kimberly picked Becky up for the teen party.

"Not a bit. Marge has several others tonight. He has a lot of playmates. He'll be fine."

"Good. And she'll have the girls' help after the dance."

Turning and with a wave of her hand, she

encouraged Jennifer to step back, surveying the Snow White costume.

"I'd say David will have competition as well."

"Speaking of Prince Charming, he's downstairs with the carriage. Are you ready?"

She took a deep breath and exhaled slowly. Her fingers trembled as she picked up the comb and with Jennifer's assistance, the teeth took hold this time. With a nod of uncertainty she gathered up her lace shawl and satin mask from the dressing table. Stephanie prayed she wasn't crossing a threshold of no return.

* * *

The weather was unseasonably warm for late October. Only a hint of the winter to come whispered in the air wafting through the open windows of the Crystal Room.

Every muscle in Brendan's body knotted in apprehension. Waiting just inside the doors of the ballroom, he curled and uncurled his fingers. Popping his knuckles wasn't a habit, yet it came involuntarily with each flex. The pop resounded in his ears. Quickly, he gripped his jacket placket. Where was Stephanie?

Having already sent the hint that she'd have to find him, he knew she would search the room. She'd never been able to refuse a challenge. Unaware of the costume he'd chosen coupled with an elaborate corn stock arrangement to hide behind, he was confident she wouldn't find him until it was time.

A hint of roses assailed his senses and he felt some of the tension leave him. Since the night she'd said yes, he'd harbored an inkling that she would change her mind, but she was here now. He only had to watch and wait. When the time was right, he would reveal himself to the Senora.

The costume she chose couldn't have been more appropriate. The old-fashioned Spanish gown paired well with his black gauchos and matching bolero jacket. Zorro was perfect both as a costume and for his plans later in the evening.

In a far corner, the band picked out a lively two-step. He watched as Jennifer and Dave joined the myriad of costume-clad guests on the dance floor, leaving Stephanie alone. His heart went out to her. She could still turn and leave but he knew she wouldn't. She'd stay and see it through. He tensed as a tall, suave Rhett Butler took Stephanie's hand in his, kissing it lightly. A wave of protectiveness raged through him. He struggled with the desire to strangle the cavalier Captain.

She laughed at something Rhett said, touching him lightly on the shoulder with her folded lace fan. Butler bowed low and sauntered off in search of a Scarlett.

Tapping her toes in time to the music, she continued to survey the room. Did she search for him? A basic animal instinct assured him of that fact and he grinned. Tonight would go just as he'd planned.

* * *

Every nerve in her body tingled. Brendan was here and he was close, very close. Surreptitiously she scanned the crowded ballroom. Of the many costumed gentlemen, only a small number could be him. Most were too short, too thin, too heavy, too fair, or a combination. After eliminating the obvious other possibilities, she had to conclude that he'd not yet arrived. Why, then, did she feel as if he stood behind her? Glancing over her left shoulder, she saw only a fall arrangement surrounded by gourds and pumpkins, but no Brendan.

"I fear Scarlett is nowhere to be found, Senora." Rhett reappeared before her. "May I have the honor of the next dance?"

"It would be a pleasure, Captain Butler." She smiled as she placed her slender gloved fingers in his large palm. Brendan could play hide and seek but Stephanie, coerced into this evening, would have a good time – with or without him.

Several partners later, she found herself thoroughly enjoying the ball. Yet with all the trips around the room, not once did she see anyone who even resembled her mystery man? Well, she wasn't going to be a wallflower for his amusement. Smilingly she accepted another invitation to dance.

Several turns later, breathless and ready for a break, she thanked her current partner then turned to leave the floor, fanning herself as she did so. Glancing around the room still searching for Brendan, she failed to see the human barrier until it was too late.

"Oh, I'm sorry. I wasn't look…"

Her breath caught as she looked up into the face

of Zorro.

The masked man said not a word. With a formal bow, he then slipped one arm around her waist, drawing her against him. Capturing her other hand in his, he propelled her into the tide of colors swirling by.

She couldn't stop staring into the eyes she knew so well as she glided in his arms. The imprint of his hand seared through the satin of her bodice, radiating through to her soul.

She felt light as air floating over the dance floor. The masked man propelled her gracefully around the ballroom to a period waltz. She was vaguely aware of the other dancers relinquishing the floor, leaving the two of them in a world of their own. As the song ended, he pulled her closer still. His breath, warm, teasing as he leaned down to whisper in her ear.

"You look ravishing, Senora. Come away with me. Together we will explore what we both have been without for too long."

Goosebumps rose in the oddest of places as she struggled to comprehend what the masked man implied. The casual placement of her hand became a life grip as desire rushed over her. Before she could reply, she felt herself swept into his strong arms and carried from the ballroom amidst cheers and laughter.

She squeaked out a feeble protest as Zorro strode out the door of the hotel. Gently, he settled her into a waiting limousine then climbed in, sitting across from her.

Darkness prevented her from seeing him clearly,

but her heart told her what her eyes could not. Indignation rose within her as she peered through the dim interior. Last she knew there were still polite ways to ask a girl out. Hauling her off the dance floor like a sack of potatoes was not one of them. Well if he wanted to play games, she'd go along. She had a thing or two in mind as well.

"Where are we going?"

The reply was nothing more than a finger to his lips and a slight nod.

"I can't be gone long, sir." She fell into his game. "I have children to look after."

"They'll be fine, Senora. I've made arrangements for their care. Tonight is ours."

They rode along in silence. She thought about asking again where they were going, but knew that the destination was all a part of his scheme.

Leaning back against the seat, she looked up through the open sunroof. The night was clear and beautiful. Millions of stars twinkled overhead. From the recesses of her mind, came the unbidden information that each star supposedly represented a loved one lost. She sent a silent prayer that Matthew would understand what she was about to do.

* * *

Traveling the short distance to the resort. Brendan watched in silence. With the exception of a mild protest, she'd taken his unspoken plan in stride. The evening breeze from the sunroof played with loose tendrils on either side of her face. She wore a relaxed smile... familiar and comforting.

What he wouldn't give to see that look every day for the rest of his life. Tonight had to work.

Gravel crunched beneath tires as the limousine came to a stop before the secluded cabin. The driver opened the door and Brendan got out, turning to extend a hand to Stephanie. Entwining his fingers with hers, he led the way up onto the covered porch and opened the cabin door.

Stepping aside, he guided her ahead of him. She stopped just within the foyer, barely allowing room for him to enter and close the door. Resting a hand on her shoulder, he waited as she took in the room before them.

Polished pine floors blended to knotty pine walls and a beamed vaulted ceiling. A native slate fireplace nestled along one wall. A warm fire glowed from behind the brass and screen guard. An overstuffed chair, ottoman, and sofa in earth tones created the invitation to relax before the hearth. Large peach roses flowed from a crystal vase on a low occasional table.

The sitting area blended into a small but efficient eat-in kitchen. A chilled bottle of sparkling cider nestled in an ornate silver ice bucket along with two fluted crystal goblets. The manager had followed his instructions to the smallest detail.

Slowly, she walked around the room, dipping her head to smell the roses, trailing her hand across the mantle, finally stopping before the dinette table. She looked at him and smiled.

"Would you care for a drink Senora?" He walked towards her. Her smile brought to mind a lighthouse beacon showing him the way home after a long journey.

"Please." Her gaze never left him and he found the task of opening the bottle of cider and pouring without spilling a trial. Brendan poured each of them a glass and handing one to her, he motioned to the sofa.

With a rustle of her gown, she tucked one leg under her as she sat down, exposing the other almost to the knee. He sat in a similar fashion, facing her. Gulping the cider as if it were stronger libation, he set his glass on the end table. Reaching for her glass, he placed it with his.

Leaning forward, he caressed her cheek with the back of his fingers. Slowly, as if petting a newborn kitten, his fingers developed a rhythm of their own. She closed her eyes, leaning into his gentle touch. He heard her sigh as she began to relax. How he'd missed her. Just the feel of her silky skin turned him inside out. This is what he'd waited and worked for all those months in treatment. To be here now...and forever.

From her cheek, he began a slow, tantalizing journey, pausing at sensuous spots along the way. Spots that he knew from another time. He brushed his thumb against her lips, feeling the tip of her tongue as she moistened them.

Ever slightly, he dipped his face to hers, applying the faintest of a kiss to the corners of her mouth. Long sustained hunger overtook him as he claimed her lips fully with his own. His tongue slipped past the moan of pleasure as she came to him in complete surrender to the emotions buried deep within.

Rising from the sofa, he pulled Stephanie up and led her to the spacious bedroom. An ornate, Victorian brass bed stood against one wall. A large Jacuzzi tub fit nicely beneath a picture window that offered a spectacular view of Beaver Lake.

"Steph?" He turned to face her, the question barely a whisper.

Unspoken, she slid her hands up his chest under the bolero, pushing it out of the way. Her gaze never leaving his face as the jacket became a pool at his feet. He smiled in amusement as she grasped the placket of the shirt and ripped it open to the waist. He felt branded where her fingers grazed as she pulled the shirttails from their haven.

As his shirt floated to the floor, Brendan tangled his fingers through her hair, loosening the comb. With devilish intent, his angel trailed fluttering kisses across his ribs and down his belly. The muscles convulsed at the torture. He heard her laugh softly with the control she possessed. Pulling back, he tilted her chin, losing himself in the passion-filled sapphire pools.

Forcing himself to a control he didn't feel Brendan dipped his lips to hers. They parted invitingly and her tongue touched his. She kissed him with a hunger as he guided them to the bed.

With a slow, deliberate movement she ran the tips of her fingers along his chest. He felt his muscles ripple like waves beneath her exquisite torment. In that moment he realized this is the way their times together should have been. Things would be different now. He would be the man she deserved.

Holding her in the aftermath of lovemaking, he kissed her tousled hair. Quiet tears dampened his chest as she buried her face close to him. His arms encircled her protectively. It wrenched him to the core for her to go through this but he knew it was a part of the acceptance. Tonight she'd taken the first big step in putting her life with Matthew behind her. With a loving caress, he let her cry until her breathing told him she slept.

"I love you Stephanie Douglas. I always have and always will." She mumbled something in her sleep, snuggling closer. With a sigh of contentment, he slipped off to join his angel in satiated slumber.

CHAPTER 9

Stephanie took a drink of the lukewarm tea. Wearing Brendan's billowy costume shirt, she sat on the porch swing in the predawn hour gazing out across the cloud-like mist covering the lake. The view calmed her thoughts. Thoughts of what she had done last night.

They'd made love several times throughout the night. Finally groaning in resistance, Brendan playfully pinned her to him with an arm of tempered steel. Within moments she'd felt his even breathing against her neck.

She knew last night hadn't been a dream. Either she'd died and gone to heaven, or been propelled into hell, she wasn't sure which exactly. She did know she had crossed the bridge of no return and she had decisions to make. She loved him beyond reason, always had if she'd be honest. Love and trust went hand in hand and that meant he was entitled to know everything. Giving him her all meant no secrets. How was she going to tell him?

"Tell me what?"

She jumped at the question, unaware she'd voiced her own. Looking from his devilish grin down to his toes, her eyes widened at the sight of him.

"Brendan, you're… I mean."

His laughter echoed across the valley.

"Naked? My angel, if we made love here on the deck, your cries of pleasure resounding through the trees, not a soul would know."

He sat on the swing next to her as if he were fully dressed for dinner. Putting an arm around her shoulders and drawing her close, he dropped a kiss onto her temple. She closed her eyes, reveling in his nearness. Curling up within the circle of his arms was as comforting now as it had been last night and all those years ago. Would it still feel the same in another ten? Maybe the better question is if he'd still be around? She wanted to believe that once he learned the truth, it wouldn't matter.

"You're very quiet." He spoke just above a whisper. "Not regretting last night, I hope."

In answer, she reached up to entwine her fingers with his across her shoulder brushing her lips where they met.

Following their first explosive reunion and a brief nap, they'd moved to the Jacuzzi tub. Amidst the musky vanilla bubbles, they'd touched, teased, and tantalized one another. Renewed discoveries took them to another level of intense passion, sending water onto the floor. She couldn't remember the last time she'd felt so content.

"What would you like to do today? We have the whole day."

"As much as I'm enjoying this, I really need to go home. Max has never woken up without me there."

"He's fine, sweetheart. The kids stayed at Jennifer's last night. He adores her."

"I know. Jen's really been a big help. I don't know what we'd have done without her when we came down here."

"When did you know she was my daughter?" With his free hand he drew an invisible pattern on her exposed thigh nearest him.

"Within a couple months of coming to Eureka Springs. I had stopped by her office to discuss reserving the ballroom for my first client. I must have been staring at the picture on her desk because she interrupted what she was saying to tell me who you were.

"Why didn't you let on about us?"

"What was I supposed to say? 'How nice. Oh by the way, I'm the one who picked out that puppy you got for Christmas that year'."

She felt him jerk away.

"What's wrong with that?" His voice trembled as he turned to face her.

"If she didn't know, then you wouldn't find out I was here." She felt the tears well up. She couldn't remember crying this much since Matthew's death. "I just prayed that when you did visit your daughter, I wouldn't have cause to run into you."

"Why?"

"Because I still loved you. I didn't need that

complication in my life...still don't."

"What about last night? Doesn't that change things between us?"

The plea in his voice tore at her heart. She wanted to tell him it changed everything, but how without divulging the secret that became heavier each day he was here?

"Last night was incredible." She leaned back against his shoulder, hoping the strength she desperately needed would flow from him.

"But?"

"Everything I do has to involve my children. Kimberly and Max are my life and our life is here."

"I know that. Haven't you figured out how I feel about you and the kids?"

"I know how you think you feel, but caring about them and being a solid form in their life are two very different things."

"You mean my touring, don't you? Steph, I can't change who I am or what I do. Entertaining is my job. It's how I would provide for our family."

The undertones of the conversation closed in around her. She stood and walked past him to the railing, searching to divert the subject.

"You know what I'd really like to do today?" She turned to him, attempting a smile.

"What? Anything you'd like."

She saw a shadow cross his face. They weren't finished with the subject. And as badly as he wanted to continue, she knew he wouldn't. For that, she loved him all the more.

"Shop. I can't remember the last time I went to the grocery store without children. And I've been thinking of new furniture for Max's room. Care to give me a masculine opinion?""I'd be happy to, but first…"

Before she fully realized his intent, he was standing again and gathering her into his arms all in one swift movement and carried her back inside the cabin.

* * *

"Jen, how much can you tell me about Steph's life prior to Eureka Springs?"

He and Steph had spent the day as she'd requested. They had found the perfect furniture befitting a young boy leaving his baby years behind. By this time next week Max would be sleeping in a real twin bed decked out in Bob the Builder bedding. After scheduling the furniture delivery, they'd nearly filled the back of the jeep with their stop at the grocery store. For the afternoon, they'd been a 'couple'. She'd asked his opinion on furniture and they'd agreed on many things. Later, pushing the cart through the supermarket as she made savvy choices, he felt as if he'd come home.

"She doesn't talk about herself much. I know that she and Matthew were very happy and that Matthew…."

"Matthew what?" Brendan watched as his daughter twisted a strand of hair around her finger. He remembered Kimberly doing that. The two must spend a lot of time together for them to have the same habits. Knots formed in the pit of his stomach. Was there something about Matthew that Stephanie hadn't told him? He'd pictured them as the perfect family.

"He was a great dad for Kimberly.

Brendan felt the zing. He knew Jennifer missed that part of her life. Debbie had chosen not to marry. He'd never understood why.

After finishing school, Debbie worked for her uncle, a prominent attorney. Taking Debbie under his wing, she'd worked as his personal secretary. As her uncle climbed the legal ladder, he'd taken her with him - all the way to the Governor's Mansion. Garrett had been a good man, caring for Debbie and Jennifer in Brendan's stead.

"I'm sorry Jen." He tucked his thumbs into his front jean pockets, balancing the chair he sat in on two legs. "I can't make up or redo any of the mistakes I made."

Jennifer unceremoniously plopped into her desk chair. Kicking off the gray pumps, she stretched and wiggled her toes as she ran long, slender fingers through her hair.

"I know Dad, and it's okay. I grew up and came to terms with all of that a long time ago."

He watched as she leaned forward. Picking up a small photo frame, she handed it to him. Taking the frame, he gazed at the three smiling faces of Stephanie and the kids.

"I just hate to see you make the same mistake. Kimberly… and Max needs a father. They want you."

Gently, he placed the frame back on the desk. "I'm working on it, okay?"

"Okay. So, what are your plans for after my

wedding? Are you laying out another tour?"

"I'm not sure." Six weeks ago he'd have answered yes. The bus would be warming up as he walked his daughter down the aisle. Now, he just didn't know. Entertaining was how he made a living, but he'd found Stephanie. He didn't want to lose her again. And she'd made it abundantly clear he couldn't be a rambler, a husband, and a father.

"That ball is in Stephanie's court. Halloween showed her how I feel. But I think there's something she's not telling me."

Brendan watched a smile play across his daughter's face before she spoke.

"Was Steph good with surprises?"

"Was she ever! She kept a secret as if her life depended on it. Why do you ask?"

Jennifer checked her watch. Brendan knew evasion when he saw it.

"We have to get to the school if we want her speaking to either one of us."

Slipping her shoes back on, she stood to gather her jacket and purse from the coat tree. He rose and helped her into the jacket.

"Why do you ask?" He repeated his question as he held open the door. "About Stephanie keeping secrets, I mean?"

"She still can." She smiled as she reached up and kissed him on the cheek before going to the elevator, leaving him to stare after her as he closed the office door.

They arrived at the high school amidst a flurry of activity. He maneuvered the jeep into what appeared to be the only available parking space left.

Inside the school, Jennifer went to the gym to assist the Pep Squad in their babysitting endeavors. Brendan followed the throng of parents and older students to the shop. Passing through the doorway mimicked the effect of stepping into another dimension.

Christmas music rang from the intercom system. Oil paint and turpentine mixed with spice and citrus permeated the room. Every head in the room sported either a Santa hat or an elf stocking. Whiskers Dan's creations covered every table, awaiting paint. Stephanie stood in the center of the activity. Her back was to him as she talked to the woodcarver.

"Hi Brendan," Kimberly and Becky greeted in unison from their table nearest the door. A chorus of greetings followed like a wave through the room.

He acknowledged the workers with a wave and a smile, never taking his eyes from Stephanie. In the wake of greetings, she turned towards the door. He watched as she made her way through the maze of tables, enjoying the rhythmic sway of her hips. Dressed in jeans and a red sweatshirt proclaiming I Believe in Santa, she looked every bit the part of the head elf in Santa's Workshop.

"This is a surprise."

"Why is that? If Eureka Springs is to be my home then I have a stake in the Santa Club, too."

Brendan watched the emotions flash across her face at the word 'home'. Had he really said that? Home was a place you came back to. But he knew that's not what he meant. Without realizing it, he cemented what he had told her at the cabin. This is where he wanted to be for the rest of his life.

"Well, we can always use the help. Are you still handy in the kitchen?" She stepped back, allowing a couple more students to enter the already packed classroom. "We're pretty full here, as you can see. Want to check in with the Booster Club on the lunch progress?"

"Lead the way." He grinned as he motioned for her to precede him into the hall.

* * *

By the end of the day every toy sported two thin coats of paint in an array of bright colors. Over the next week, shop class students would put a coat of sealer on them. Home Ec. students had the job of carefully wrapping and tagging each one in preparation for delivery on Christmas Eve.

"How do you distribute all of these toys?" He shouldered a dozing Max as he followed her to the car.

"On Christmas Eve, Santa and an elf ride through the countryside in a horse drawn sleigh or wagon, depending on the weather."

"Amazing. Do I dare ask who plays the part of Santa?"

"Plays?" Her eyes twinkled with merriment. "Why Santa himself, of course."

Pointing to her shirt he asked, "Do you believe in Santa?"

"I believe in what he stands for." She opened the car door, then stood aside as he buckled Max into the car seat. She looked up at the overcast sky.

Chances were good they'd have snow before the week began.

"What's that?" He backed out of the car and she shut the door as quietly as possible so as not to wake Max. If she were lucky, she could tuck him into bed without being up half the night with a recharged little boy.

"Caring more for someone else than yourself. Giving from your heart, not because it's expected. Believing that anything is possible."

"What do you want for Christmas, Angel?"

The question cut her to the bone. She knew what she wanted more than anything. What she prayed for would take…

"A miracle. What about you? Expecting coal in your stocking?"

"I've been a good boy. I get whatever I want."

"Oh really."

That had been her problem. She had always let Brendan have his way. As soon as he'd kissed her and his hands began to roam, she had caved. Just like at the cabin.

"And what is it that you've asked Santa for?"

"We'll have to see Christmas morning." He bent to kiss her soft and undemanding. Before she was able to reciprocate, he walked away, whistling Jingle Bells.

Shaking her head in amusement, she got in the car for the short drive home.

CHAPTER 10

"Bedan." Max squealed, running in the front door of Borderline Studios towards him.

"Hey, buddy." He caught the toddler up in his arms and settled him against a shoulder. Holding the boy with one arm, he pulled Kimberly into an embrace with the other.

"Hi, kiddo."

"Hi, Brendan."

When she hugged him back, a feeling of acceptance tugged at his heart.

After much persuasion, Jennifer agreed to bring the kids to Branson. Being a father meant that Stephanie wouldn't always be there every minute. He needed to reassure himself that he could attend to their needs without her looking on. What better way than being totally responsible for them an entire day? It didn't compare to real life, but it would have to do.

"Is this where you cut your records?" Kimberly

stepped away from him.

He watched as she walked around the lobby. She read the plate engravings labeling each gold and platinum album lining the walls. Her familiar brown eyes danced in awe. She was going to be a heartbreaker.

"First time I've used this studio. Nashville has been my recording home until now. Would you like to see the place?"

"Would I? You bet!"

"I put a change of clothes in the jeep for Max, just in case." Jennifer kissed Brendan on the cheek "I still don't like this. Stephanie is going to have my head if, no make that when she finds out. You have my cell number if you need anything."

"Thanks. We'll be fine." Brendan looked to the kids for support. "Won't we kids?"

"Yep." Max gave a sharp nod of his head.

"Where are we meeting later?" Jennifer paused at the door.

"Barney's Burger Palace around six. Okay with you?"

"Works for me, Dad. I'll see you then."

After she left, Brendan put Max down to walk. Their slow pace allowed his little legs to keep up as they toured the suite of offices. The secretaries fell in love with the cherub faced child. One offered to occupy his 'son' while Kim finished the tour. He didn't correct the secretary's mistake. If everything went as planned, there'd be nothing to correct.

A close friend of his currently used one of the booths. Kimberly nearly burst with excitement at being able to listen in on a recording. When the session broke up, she asked in-depth questions about everything, making constructive comments. He marveled at how she picked up on the technical things. He would have to talk to Stephanie about letting Kim spend time at the studio while he worked on this album. She would get a kick out of it and they would have more time to get to know one another.

"Brendan, I need your help." They'd left the studio and were buckling up in the jeep in search of the next adventure.

"Sure. If I can."

"I want to buy Mom something special for Christmas."

"What do you have in mind?" He glanced in her direction before pulling out into the infamous Branson traffic.

"I'm not sure." Her brow furrowed in concentration. "It has to be really cool. I thought you might have some ideas."

"I have a birthday present to buy for you know who." He motioned to the back seat where Max was intent on one of the picture books from his tote bag. "I have no clue what to get. Let's put our heads together over a banana split. We'll help each other out."

"Thanks. I knew I could count on you." The smile she gave cast a glow within him. He only hoped he didn't let her down.

For the remainder of the afternoon, the threesome wandered through a variety of outlet shops and played miniature golf. With her help, he knew what to get Max for his birthday. With that out of the way, they continued their search for the perfect gift for Stephanie.

"How about this Kimberly?" He shifted a dozing boy on his shoulder. Getting Kim's attention, he pointed to a white pillar candle.

Carefully, she took the large candle off the shelf. Standing about eight inches tall, the candle was at least four inches in diameter. Different from others in the shop, this one wasn't for burning. A small clear votive cup set down inside the hollow center.

"Have you seen these before?" A voice came from behind them. Kimberly turned to the lady, shaking her head.

"Watch this." She smiled as she took an LED tea-light candle from her smock pocket. She moved the switch on the bottom into position then set it inside the votive cup. A silhouette of an angel glowed through the side of the pillar. Opalescent wings glittered in the firelight.

"It's beautiful. Mom would love it." Her smile out shown the candle's glow. "How much is it?"

"$23.95 plus tax. Gift wrapping is free."

He watched the crestfallen look come over Kimberly. Slowly, she put the candle back on the shelf.

"If you're short, I can help?"

"No, that's okay. I'll keep looking."

Her tone was solemn and his heart constricted with a pain he couldn't describe. He had never wanted to be a champion for anyone as much as he did for this young woman.

"Kim, you're a Girl Scout, right?"

"Yeah."

"Do you remember the Brownie elf story?"

"Sure. Mom taught me a long time ago. Brownie elves help others with tasks. Kind of in secret."

"Well I'd like to be an elf, but I need some help. If you help me, I'll pay you – in advance."

"But elves don't take money. They do it because they want to."

"Exactly. Can we trade favors?"

He watched as she weighed the decision, seeing Stephanie's independence.

"Okay. But you have to promise that I truly get to help you in return."

"Scouts Honor." He held up a three-finger salute.

"Wonderful." The sales lady smiled at the decision. "I have one back here that hasn't been tested. "I'll make sure it's okay while you select the wrapping."

Minutes later, the clerk gave the bow a final tug and rang up the sale.

"Sign here, please." She handed him the charge slip. "Your daughter's very pretty. And this guy is a cutie."

"He's not my Dad. But I wish he was." Brendan almost missed her final words uttered in a barely audible whisper.

"Really?" The sales lady handed him the card and receipt. "You look just like him. I apologize for my error, Mr. Keane."

"It's okay." He put the credit card and slip in his wallet while trying not to disturb Max. He wasn't successful.

"Eat?"

"Sure buddy. Let's head to Barney's." He turned

to Kim. "Ready to go?"

Her eyes had lost their sparkle as she took the package and headed for the door without answering.

Walking back to the jeep, Brendan pondered the lady's comments. He'd never given a lot of thought to how little Kimberly resembled her Mom. He just assumed she took more after Matthew. Something else tapped at his brain like Morse code. What was he missing?

They made the drive to Barney's in a deafening silence. Jennifer waited inside the doors. He saw the questioning look and shook his head, hoping she understood. Once they were settled in a booth, the only time Kim spoke was to place her order. When her food arrived, she picked at more than she ate.

Brendan felt Jennifer nudge him in the arm.

"What's up with her?" Her tone was barely audible.

Brendan gave her the 'not now' look again as he squirted more catsup for Max.

He hadn't heard a word from the sullen teenager since leaving the store. While the hope of the kids accepting him as a father had been a part of today's plan, Kim's soft-spoken wish had hit him like a wrecking ball. If things didn't work out between him and Stephanie, those six words would haunt him forever.

"Jennifer, would you take Max into the play land?" He motioned to the toddler, running a finger through the catsup on his plate.

"Sure. Let's go play, Max." She stood and held out her hand.

"Bedan too."

"You go play buddy. I want to talk to sissy."

Sensing protest, Jennifer caught his attention with a challenge. "Come on Max, I'll race you."

That's all it took to distract him as he shot ahead to the door.

"Want to talk about it?"

She shook her head as he watched her bottom lip quiver.

"It's okay. Every kid should have a dad."

"I had a dad. He was great." Her outburst sent the tears falling onto cold French fries. "But he isn't here and I miss him."

Brendan took the partially eaten burger she still clutched and put it down. Taking both of her hands in one large one, he tilted her chin with the other.

"I know you do sweetheart. You'll always miss him."

"Mom does too."

"She loved your dad. He will always be a part of all of you."

"Do you love my mom?"

Letting go of her hands, he sat back in the booth. How could he answer that without misleading her or raising hopes? Trusting eyes never left his face as he strove to find the right words.

"Has your mom ever mentioned knowing me before she married your dad?"

She shook her head.

"It's true. Your mom and I dated before she met him."

"Really?" Her eyes widened in disbelief. "What happened?"

"I wasn't ready for marriage and a family. Your

mom wanted a family and a home so I became a part of her past."

Kimberly picked up the cold burger and took a bite. He watched as she appeared to mull over the information.

"Can we go home now?" She tossed the burger back onto the plate.

"Sure. Why don't you go get the rest of the crew? I'll clean up here."

As Jennifer's Neon disappeared down the strip, Brendan got in his jeep and drove back to the studio. In his office, he quickly dialed Planned to Perfection. He hadn't meant for Stephanie to find out about today this way but she needed to warn her. He sensed a storm headed her direction.

Unladylike words rang in his ears minutes later as he hung up the phone. Leaning back in the office chair and propping his feet on the corner of the desk, he stared at a picture of Jennifer. The comments of the sales lady pealed through his mind. 'Just like you...just like you', raced faster and faster until his head hurt.

Was Kimberly his daughter? Surely Stephanie would have told him. Or would she? He'd have still been a drunk then. He tried to calculate the possibility but his brain refused to cooperate. Slowly, the things he'd witnessed over the past few weeks began to make sense. Things like the way both girls twirled their hair in nervousness. They had his brown eyes while Stephanie's were blue. He got up, nearly capsizing the chair in haste. Something told him he should be at Stephanie's when that storm hit.

* * *

Fear coursed through Stephanie as she disconnected the call. Brendan had been with Jennifer and the kids. He just wanted to let her know they were on their way home. The possibilities of what could have happened pulled at her like an undertow.

At home she could protect Kimberly, but in close proximity for several hours, he was bound to notice the similarities between their daughters. Thankfully, Jennifer knew and that was the only protection she had today. She should have told him. In her heart, she knew the news couldn't wait any longer. Once the initial shock passed, she felt he'd understand. It wasn't like he could try for custody or anything.

She stumbled back against the counter as a new shockwave crashed through her. Sourness rose from the pit of her stomach. The idea that he might attempt such a thing hammered through her mind. She had not thought of that possibility. Legally could he do that? Would she be able to prevent him from gaining even shared custody? Kimberly had been born a Douglas. Surely that would carry weight in a court of law.

Matthew was the only father the girl had ever known. He'd loved her as his own and she adored him in return. There'd never been a reason to tell her otherwise. Now she would have to.

Oh Lord, what a mess. All she wanted was a home and family. Matthew had provided that unconditionally. Never in her wildest dreams had she anticipated having Brendan back in her life.

Voices in the front hall interrupted her thoughts. Smoothing her trousers and forcing a smile, Stephanie left the kitchen, reaching them just as Jennifer started upstairs with Max.

"You wore him out, I see?" She pointed, not letting on what she knew. He nestled against her friend oblivious to the disaster about to shake his world. Yes, this would affect him as well. The three of them were a package deal. Brendan would have to make the choice to accept it or not.

"I'll put him down."

"Thanks Jennifer. Then I'd like to talk to you." She turned to Kimberly. "Did you have fun?"

"It was okay." Her tone gave Stephanie every indication that things hadn't gone well.

"Brendan showed me the studio and stuff. I think I'll go to bed."

"Alright sweetheart. You can tell me about it tomorrow."

She watched her daughter slowly climb the stairs. Something had snuffed out the girl's sparkle and exuberance. The light was gone. She heard the bedroom door click shut just as Brendan came into the foyer.

"You," she whirled on him. "In my office." Brushing past him, she left no room for refusal. "Just what did you think you were doing?" The fear she'd felt at Brendan's phone call multiplied a hundred times at the sight of her daughter moments before.

"I just wanted some time with the kids. Alone."

"You couldn't ask? You had to sneak behind my

back?" Her voice sounding shrill, even to her own ears.

"I should have asked. I'm sorry."

"Sorry? What happened?" She used every fiber of her being to force her voice to a semi-normal point. "Why is she going to her room at eight o'clock on a Saturday night?"

"It's been a long day. We did a lot of shopping."

"Steph, it was my fault," Jennifer joined them in the office. "I didn't tell you my plans and I apologize."

"How could you?" Her voice cracked with emotion she tried desperately to hide. "You of all people knew what was at stake."

"Dad just wanted some time with the kids. Under the circumstances I knew you'd never agree to it."

"It wasn't your call to make."

"I know and I'm sorry."

"What circumstances?"

Stephanie felt like a participant in a game of Hot Potato and he'd just passed it to her. The blood pounded in her ears and her mouth went dry. The words wouldn't come.

"I'm going to leave. You two have things to talk about. Call me tomorrow if you want."

Stephanie wasn't entirely aware of Jennifer's exit. Walking over to the collection of photos, she picked up one of Matthew in uniform. Laughing blue eyes stared back, his smile confidant. He'd been her strength when she realized she was pregnant. They had talked long into the night. He didn't judge her, just held her while she cried. She'd been confused but not alone. He knew the baby wasn't his and loved her anyway. From that moment on, Kimberly had become his daughter.

Clutching the photo to her breast, she turned back to Brendan. He sat at her desk, watching her. Just like the old days, he waited for her to talk when she felt ready. How many nights had he sat silently, waiting for her to tell him what was on her mind?

"We need to talk."

"I know."

"Mom, can I talk to you?" Kimberly stood timidly in the doorway, twirling her hair tightly around a finger. Stephanie looked from Brendan to her daughter.

"Sure honey, come in. What's wrong?"

"I'll leave you two alone. We'll continue this later."

"No Brendan!" Kimberly snapped. "Stay."

"Kimberly. Don't be rude. I think you owe him an apology."

"If anyone owes him an apology, Mom, it's you." Her daughter walked over to stand beside him. Tears welled up in the girl's eyes and her bottom lip trembled as she tried to control whatever was upsetting her.

"Sweetheart, what's the matter?" She reached out. Kimberly took a step back.

"Brendan, please stay. I want you to hear this."

Kimberly reached out a shaking hand and placed it on his shoulder. A burning sensation ate at Stephanie from the inside. Fear grew inside of her, creeping along her spine as she looked from her daughter, to Brendan and back again.

"Sounds serious Kim. What is it?"

Kimberly glanced at Brendan for a moment before turning to face her.

"Mom, is Brendan my real dad?"

CHAPTER 11

"Mom, I need to know. He's my dad, isn't he?"

Stephanie looked from daughter to father and back again. Nodding her head, she couldn't stop the flow of tears sliding down her face. It shouldn't have come to this. Two of the people she loved the most sat staring in muted disbelief. Kimberly stepped slowly across the office to stand before her. Stephanie reached out and touched the young girl's face.

"Since before you were born, Matthew has been your father. We never meant for it to be any other way."

"Did you know?" Kimberly looked at Brendan.

"No." Stephanie didn't wait for him to answer. "He didn't know. Not until now."

She handed Matthew's photo to Kimberly.

"This is the man who watched you come into this world. The same man who helped you take your first step, taught you to ride your bike, and to swim in the lake."

"I'd have done those things Stephanie."

The fortress Stephanie had built around her secret crumbled a little more at the accusing tone in Brendan's voice as he joined them in the center of the room. She had never given him the chance. That was on her.

"Like you were there for Jennifer? That's why I didn't tell you about the baby."

Angry tears came in a torrent. How dare either of them make her feel as if she'd done something wrong? She had done what she needed to do to protect her daughter. Matthew had been the knight in shining armor, offering her a kingdom of security. Security Brendan hadn't understood at the time.

"You wouldn't change for me or for her. One more on the list wasn't going to make a difference."

"Neither you nor Debbie gave me the chance." His hardened tone stabbed her to the bone, but he didn't stop there. "Each of you made the decision to exclude me from my girls' lives."

"Because you weren't capable of making them."

"Well it beat the alternative."

"What? Facing life? You had me, Brendan, but you drank anyway! But then, you never did claim to love me. Some things don't change."

The quiet undertone of a raging storm fueled her emotions.

"Are you going to deal with this or would you prefer a drink?"

She'd gone too far. The wounded look in his eyes chiseled at the fragmented wall around her heart, yet she couldn't stop the tirade. She hurt too much--for all of them.

"Oh yeah, I forgot. You learned how to face your problems in Program. Did they also counsel you in how to raise children?"

"That's not fair, Steph."

The slamming of the front door sounded like gunfire.

"Kimberly!" Stephanie screamed her daughter's name as she ran to the hallway. Brendan was close behind her. Opening the door, she frantically looked up and down the street. There was no sign of her daughter. "Kimmie." Only the darkness replied.

Turning back into the house, she shut the door with as much force as the angry teen.

"Now do you see why I didn't want you here? Why couldn't you have just done the Gala then quietly left town?"

"Because I wanted to spend time with Jennifer. Last I checked the map, this town is still a part of free America."

"I'll call Becky's. I'm sure she's gone there." She pushed past him, going over to the desk. She slumped down into the chair and picked up her cell phone. Only a couple of minutes passed before she disconnected and looked at Brendan.

"She hasn't seen Kim."

"Where else would she go?"

She shrugged her shoulders helplessly. "I don't know. Becky's really the only one she is close to."

"Why don't you give it some thought while I make tea? I could use a cup."

"I don't want tea! I want to know where my

daughter is."

"Our daughter. I'm concerned too, but we'll find her."

After Brendan left the room, Stephanie leaned on the desk, covering her face with her hands. She needed to think. Where could Kimberly have gone if not to her best friend?

She grabbed the phone before it had completed the first ring. "Kim? Oh...Jennifer. Is she okay? I'll be right there, thanks."

"Was that Kimberly?" Brendan came back into the room and sat the tea tray on the desk as Stephanie stood to leave.

"No, it was Jen. Kim's with her."

"I'll come with you." He grabbed their coats from the hall tree.

"No. I need someone here with Max."

"Then let me go. You can't leave me out of her life anymore."

"This is different Brendan. You and I will talk later but right now my daughter has questions that only I can answer."

She saw the hesitation in his eyes as well as the resignation that followed. He and Kim would have their time to sift through the mess she had kept locked away for years. Right now, no matter how mad she was, Kim needed her mom.

"Fine."

The drive up to the Crescent didn't take long. Apparently, she had headed for Jennifer's cottage but when she didn't see the car in the small parking area, she'd walked the rest of the way to the hotel where Jennifer was finishing up some things at the office.

Jennifer opened the door to Stephanie's light knock. She stepped aside and motioned to the Queen Anne sofa on the opposite side of the room. Stephanie was vaguely aware of Jennifer leaving. All she could focus on was the little girl huddled against the back of the sofa, clutching a throw pillow to her chest and staring at the picture she'd brought from the house. Her eyes were puffy from crying. With cautious steps, Stephanie made her way across the room and sat next to Kimberly.

"Why'd you marry Dad?"

"Because he asked. Because he wanted to take care of us."

"Did you love him?"

Her daughter wasn't pulling any punches with this conversation. While Stephanie had always seen Kimberly as mature for her age, she hadn't expected this conversation at least until she thought her daughter was old enough in age to understand all the complexities of the puzzle that was her life. She had known there would be lots of questions and she had spent what seemed a lifetime preparing for them. Did she love Matthew wasn't one she had considered.

"Yes, I did. Honey, there are different kinds of love. The best way I can define the two I felt is that Brendan was a 'young love', the kind that makes you go all mushy inside."

"What about Dad?" Kimberly continued to stare at the picture, never looking at Stephanie.

"With him it was more mature. We liked the same things and we were friends. He was ready to settle down and start a family."

"Why didn't you tell Brendan about me?"

As they talked, Kim slowly came out of the fetal position and for the first time in several hours, Stephanie sensed things might work out.

"Brendan wasn't ready to quit drinking and grow up. Not having a mom of my own to ask advice, I followed Debbie's example."

"You mean about her parents not letting him be a dad to Jennifer?"

She nodded. "The more I looked at the whole picture, I figured her folks knew best."

"I don't mean this the way it's gonna sound but…"

Stephanie watched as her daughter's cheeks flushed a bright crimson. "But…?"

"How'd you know which one was my dad?"

The question was barely audible. Her little girl was growing up so fast. She had given the situation a lot of thought in a very short time.

"Matthew wanted to wait until we were married. Brendan was the only man I'd ever been with."

"Did you ever plan to tell me?"

"Your Dad and I'd talked about it. We decided that as far as we were concerned, he was your father. Until a few months ago, I never imagined you'd ever need to know any different. But we were wise enough to know that if this did come up, we had hoped you'd be older."

"Do you still love Brendan?" Kimberly asked, twisting a strand of hair around her finger.

"Boy, you ask the tough questions." Stephanie attempted to lighten the somber cloud that hung over the room. How did she answer that without belittling the love they'd shared with Matthew? Deciding it was time to take a lesson from Brendan, she answered her daughter the only way there was… with honesty.

"Yes, I do but that doesn't change the way I loved your father. My heart has room for both of them."

"Nothing personal Mom, but I don't need any more surprises like the one I got tonight. I just want to know what's going to happen next. I mean, is Brendan going to be my Dad or what?"

Reaching across to Kimberly, Stephanie removed the pillow and took her daughter's hands in hers.

"I honestly don't know. Brendan has his own questions I'm going to have to answer. What do you think should happen?"

Kimberly's eyes pooled with tears again. Taking a tissue from the box on the table, she wiped at her eyes and sniffled.

"I really miss Dad and I know you do too. Max has never had a father and he likes Brendan. No one can take Dad's place but I'd like to get to know Brendan better."

"Sounds fair. For now, I think we need to go home. Brendan's waiting and we've all had a long day."

"Mom?" Kim stood, wiping the remaining dampness from her cheeks.

"Hmm?"

"I'm sorry I ran off. You guys were arguing and it was like I didn't exist."

"I know sweetie. I'm sorry too."

* * *

For what must have been the hundredth time, Brendan peered out the window as Stephanie's SUV pulled up to the curb. He opened the door.

"Thanks." Stephanie said, taking off her coat and hanging it up. "Everything okay here?"

"Uh huh. Max hasn't made a sound. I checked on him a couple times."

"Good."

"Brendan."

"Kimmy." They both spoke at once and then laughed. Brendan felt an immense relief. Kim's ability to laugh after the way the evening had started out was a good sign.

"You go first." He said.

"No, you."

"I just wanted to say I'm sorry about earlier. The news caught me off guard."

"I know, me too. I'm sorry I ran off."

He returned the hug she gave and sent a silent prayer of thanks that she still wanted to.

"You guys have to talk and I'm beat. I'm going to bed. Night Mom, night...Brendan."

Their chorused good night gave Brendan the feeling of hope. Their voices in unison sounded natural. They were parents telling their pre-teen daughter to sleep well as if they too would be going upstairs. The thought that the possibility lay ahead somewhere made him smile.

"I'm ready for that cup of tea now." Stephanie

turned to walk down the hall towards the kitchen. "Want some?"

"Sure. I'll help. I've already cleaned up from earlier. We'll need to start fresh."

Breathing a sigh of relief, he followed her. Starting fresh sounded like a good plan. When she'd gone after Kim earlier, he didn't have a clue what to expect when they returned. Stephanie wasn't throwing him out, leaving hope for the two of them.

Stephanie didn't say anything as she busied herself getting cups and spoons. He heard her movements as he put the teakettle on. Waiting for it to whistle, he leaned against the kitchen counter, watching her.

Something in the back of his mind, like a forgotten photograph flashed through his mind. He vaguely remembered her fixing dinner for him one night. He'd come home from work, thinking to take a quick shower before heading across the bridge to his favorite bar. She'd been there, her hair in a ponytail and an apron tied around her waist as she sat the table for dinner. She'd given the impression of a 1950s housewife. That was the only time he could remember not going to the bar after work. He couldn't recall what she had prepared or if they even ate. He only remembered dessert.

Setting a place for each of them, she then selected the tea packets. He smiled with chagrin, noticing she chose the exact same two varieties he had the night of the art club meeting. Even after all these years, they knew each other well; their likes and dislikes. They probably discovered more about each other in these past two months than they'd ever truly known about each other the three plus years they'd been together. So how had he missed the most important information all those years ago? The answer was simple. He hadn't been drinking tea then. She knew him then and now. Thirteen years ago he wouldn't have been anymore ready to be a dad to Kim then he'd been to Jennifer. Stephanie made the only choice she could. Now it was his turn.

Pouring water into their cups, he put the kettle back on the stove then sat across from her at the table.

"Now what?" He couldn't bring himself to look at Stephanie, instead focused on stirring a spoon of sugar into his tea.

"What do you mean?"

He still wasn't sure how to react. He'd known deep inside what he'd find at the eye of the storm. On the drive from Branson and while he'd waited for Stephanie to bring Kim home, he'd thought about the whole situation.

"I can't leave the road. You know that."

"Then nothing's changed."

"I told you before, it's how I make a living."

"And the children are my life."

"She's my daughter, too." How could he get through to her? He wanted...no, needed this chance. Having the opportunity to raise a child was the one part of recovery he'd never dreamed of being able to correct. A tragic trail of events brought his life full circle. He'd prove to her that he was capable of being the father she needed for the kids.

"How does Kim feel about things?"

"She wants to get to know you."

"I'd like that, too. I've missed out on so much her life already." Brendan could barely contain his joy.

When he'd first seen Stephanie that night at the Gala, he felt as if he could finally have closure with his past and move forward. Initially his only hope was for Stephanie to forgive him. He'd never imagined that his past would be a large part of his future.

"I've got to make a short trip down to Austin for a couple days. I could do it over a weekend and take Kim with me."

"Not hardly."

"Why not? I know she gets out early on Friday. She'll love it." He began to mentally tick off all the other things they'd be able to do.

"No." The tone of finality in her voice popped the balloon of elation, raising a challenge within him.

"This isn't just about you anymore Stephanie." He spoke more firmly than he intended. Trying to control the emotions whirling within him he continued. "She's my daughter, too and I have rights."

A mask of fear covered her face yet he couldn't stop the words that followed.

"We can settle this ourselves or let the courts decide."

"You wouldn't?"

"It's your call Stephanie. One way or another I'll be a part of Kimberly's life. Think about it." Rising to leave, he stopped to kiss her cheek. "I'll call you tomorrow."

* * *

"You did what? Dad, are you nuts?"

He stood leaning against a window frame in Jennifer's office. Looking out across the valley he felt inclined to agree. He hadn't meant to bring up the possibility of settling things in court but the realization that he had another daughter blindsided him.

"You aren't seriously considering a custody battle, are you? Because if you are, I'd have to side with Stephanie on this."

Turning from the window he saw the look of apprehension on her face. Didn't he have a right to expect to be able to spend time with Kimberly? Brendan knew that he did and he wasn't going to wait until she was eighteen for it to happen. He'd been down that road before.

"You've been in her place. What do you think?"

She got up from the chair and came around to wrap her arms around his waist in a hug. "When I was twelve years old, I wished for only one thing."

"And that was?"

"For the three of us to be a family. I didn't get my wish, but you can make Kim a very happy young lady."

"Stephanie won't even consider that as long as I'm on the road. Touring is what I do and I can't give that up."

"No Dad, performing is what you do. You have alternative ways of doing that."

"Speaking of performing, I'm going down to Austin to sit in on a recording session with J.C."

"What about Thanksgiving? Or the wedding?" A hint of panic rose in her voice and she stepped back.

"It's only for a couple of days. I'll be back in time to walk you down the aisle, I promise. I just need to get away for a while." Pulling her into a hug, he kissed her on the forehead. "I love you."

"I love you too, Dad. Be careful."

CHAPTER 12

"Look what Jennifer brought you, Max." Stephanie pushed a red button on the square box. A rotund little bear popped from under the matching lid. In a child-like voice, a recording said, 'my vest is red'. "Try this one." She pointed to a different color.

"Don't want to." Max tucked his chubby little hands under his arms while his lips formed a full-on pout. "Want Bedan."

"I know sweetie. We'll see him soon." She reached over and stroked his chestnut curls, trying to comprehend her baby was now three years old.

So much had happened since the day she found out he was growing inside of her. While the rest of her world seemed off-kilter, he had become her compass on their new path. Just as Matthew had been her guide when she carried Kimberly. Like father, like son.

Because of his love and support she had not followed her heart and gone back to Brendan or told him about the baby. At the time she didn't think he was capable of changing, but she loved him. While she knew love wasn't enough, not being with him left an ache in her heart. Gradually, Matthew had changed her world.

Matthew hadn't offered her anything more than his friendship and protection. He had accepted Kimberly as his own even before she was born. The day she entered the world, he had been the first to hold her and kiss her tiny, wrinkled forehead before handing her to Stephanie. Even before that first blessing, he had become her dad and the only child he would ever know. He would have loved both of them equally.

The tantrum Max threatened now was a prime example of what she'd feared would happen. Brendan's job would take him away for weeks at a time, leaving her to clean up in the aftermath of her son's stormy moments until his return. Now that she knew the truth, Kim's attachment was understandable. She was also old enough to understand there were times when Brendan would not be around. Max was another issue. Her baby had grown attached to Brendan very quickly, being the only male to be in his life to make a connection. She couldn't explain to Max how his new best friend's life worked. She wasn't going to put either of her children through this emotional roller coaster. Brendan was going to have to make a choice.

Trying to derail an impending tantrum, she pulled another birthday present from the pile. "This one's from Kimmie."

With encouragement from his sister, he tore open

the paper to reveal a drum. Stephanie groaned audibly as he began to beat on the instrument, grinning broadly. Well, she wanted distraction.

Stephanie raised her voice above the racket. "Kimberly, you've created a monster. Why don't you take him upstairs to play while Jennifer and I finish dinner? David is trying to watch the game and I'm sure he'd appreciate being able to hear it as well."

"Okay. Come on squirt. We'll make a recording of your first performance, like Brendan does."

Gathering up the shreds of wrapping paper and bows, Stephanie took them to the garbage then began the final preparations for dinner. Jennifer was just taking the turkey from the oven.

"Hey Stephanie, sounds like Max made quite a haul."

"He liked the drums the best. Kim said your dad helped pick them out."

She knew it would take some time before she could refer to Brendan as dad where Kimberly was concerned. He had always been Jennifer's dad.

"Have you heard from him?"

Stephanie shook her head. "No, and after our last conversation, I see it as a blessing."

"He didn't mean it. Dad just wants to spend time with Kim and have a part in her life."

"I know. I just don't know the best way to go about it." She wasn't sure there was a good way. He'd proven her point by taking off for the recording session. She couldn't allow him to be around when it suited him and gone the same way. The children needed stability and routine in their lives.

"We never talked about that trip to Branson." Stephanie took a large platter from the cabinet and sat it on the counter next to the roasting pan.

She had avoided the conversation until she had the chance to sort things out. She knew Jennifer hadn't meant any harm. Maybe by agreeing to his scheme, she had been trying to please her dad as she'd not had the opportunity growing up. Stephanie gave a silent shrug as she stirred the gravy a last time then turned off the burner.

"I'm sorry. I wasn't thinking about him discovering the truth. He just wanted to see if he could do the 'dad' thing."

"You were matchmaking?" Stephanie attempted a smile.

"Mad?"

Stephanie got the gravy boat down and proceeded to fill it. "I should be." She smiled at Jennifer. She could never be mad at the young woman who had been through so much in her life and still optimistic that dreams could come true. "I guess a part of me really wanted it to work."

"There's still a chance. Have you talked to Santa?"

"Oh you." She playfully threw the potholder at her friend. "Go tell David we're ready for him to carve the bird."

The last time she had asked Santa for something, she had sat on the man's lap in their small-town pharmacy following the Christmas parade and asked him to not let her mom die. While in her heart she knew that wasn't something the pretend Santa could deliver, a small part of her had still been the girl wanting desperately to believe there was a real Santa and he could make it happen.

While she believed in what the jolly man in the red suit represented, she knew if things were to work out, she and Brendan were both going to have to give somewhere. Could he give up life on the road and find another way to keep his career on track? Would she be able to entrust him with their daughter? He had never had a hand in raising Jennifer, always the playboy bachelor turned entertainer. Would he know what to do if she got sick? Or what if she became a young woman?

Kim was nearing that age and they'd had the talk so she was as prepared as any young girl could be. Kim was better prepared than she had been when her first cycle came. But how would Brendan handle the situation? Stephanie shook her head as she picked up the gravy boat and headed for the dining room. These were things they needed to discuss when he got back. His couple of days in Austin had turned into almost two weeks.

The combination Thanksgiving and birthday dinner passed without a word from Brendan. Jennifer's attempt to lighten the somber mood fell flat. The jokes David told failed to bring the laughter response they usually received until he finally gave up. Kimberly picked at her food, surreptitiously eyeing the place where Brendan usually sat. How could one man make such a difference in such a short time? Family dinners had taken on a new life over the past few weeks.

From that first Sunday dinner invitation, he had

become a member of their circle. He always brought something to the meal and helped with the clean-up afterward. Some nights he would read a story to Max and tuck him in before joining her on the sofa for tea. All of that seemed to evaporate with the news that Kimberly was his daughter. Stephanie felt as if she'd lost another part of herself as well. Just like when Matthew died. Putting the last of the leftovers in the fridge, she turned in time to see Kimberly in the doorway. Her sullen face speaking volumes.

"Honey, he'll be back."

"I know Mom. But I keep remembering what you said."

"What nonsense thing was that?"

"About having Brendan for a Dad not being all that I thought it would be."

"What do you mean?" Stephanie paused in wiping off the counter to look at her.

"He goes on tour a lot and won't be here much. Dad tried to go to my stuff at school and he never missed a holiday dinner."

Taking the suddenly grown-up young lady's hand, Stephanie drew her to a chair. "I've done something wrong in not telling you about him." Kim started to interrupt but Stephanie raised her hand. "Let me finish. I've kept him out of your life long enough. I can't do that anymore."

"What do you mean?"

"When Brendan gets back we'll talk some more. He's right, you two do need to spend time together; see what his life is like."

"What about you? And Max? Brendan's become

like part of the family, Mom."

"I know sweetheart. I also know what you're thinking but I don't know if that will ever be possible. Let's just take this one step at a time, shall we?"

"Okay."

"Let's make some cocoa then curl up with a Christmas movie."

After Kimberly had gone to bed, Stephanie sat on the couch enjoying a second cup of cocoa. The tree they normally decorated on Thanksgiving sat dark and forlorn in the corner, mimicking her feelings.

She couldn't remember having a tree after her Mom died. Not at home. Since she spent Christmas Eve at Brendan's and the following day at his folks, the holiday tradition didn't seem important. She doubted if Dad even noticed the absence of either her or the tree. There hadn't been stockings or gifts. The one gift she had purchased for him with her tip money, a new wallet, he'd barely looked at before tossing the box on the coffee table before going into the kitchen to refill his shot glass. He always drank from a shot, thinking he was moderating his intake. By the time he'd consumed half the fifth, she was headed to Brendan's.

She and Brendan decorated a small tree, but it wasn't the same. None of the ornaments held memories. Just colored baubles to reflect the lights. He wasn't Dad in any sense, but drinking was a constant. Hanging ornaments and drinking was not a great combination but at least Brendan made it fun. While most of the glass spheres wound up on the tree, she and Brendan wore more tinsel than they hung.

For the past week, Stephanie had pondered how best to deal with Brendan's suggestion that they go to court. She knew that wasn't the way to decide what was best for their daughter. As adults, she and Brendan should be able to come to an agreement they could all live with.

On the plus side, being at the peak of his career, Brendan would be on tour a lot. That meant nothing would really change here at home. She had her job, Kimberly would be in school, and Max needed a preschool or playgroup. Brendan's visits would be few and far between.

The challenges would come when he wouldn't be on the road. Would things be as they'd been these past three months? With her going about her business and he'd drop in whenever it suited him? No, that arrangement wouldn't work. They'd have to come to some type of cohesive agreement. Visitation rights, maybe.

With a heavy sigh, she unplugged the tree and went upstairs to bed. Now if he'd just come back so they could talk. Home. His if he chose. The love she'd had for Brendan all those years ago had aged like a fine wine. A part of her still yearned for the 'mushy' love she'd explained to Kimberly. But the mature woman in her wanted a man to love and hold again. One who would love her in return; caring for her and the children as Matthew had done. Not just any man would do. Her heart had always belonged to Brendan. He'd been gone only a couple of weeks and already she felt his absence.

She'd spent most of her adult life missing him and it wasn't how she wanted to grow old.

* * *

"Sounded good. I think I like using the steel guitar better than the flat top." Brendan clipped his mic back into the holder.

He'd been in Austin with J.C. a couple of weeks producing the new album. As long as he was in the studio, Brendan could focus on the music instead of Stephanie, but the off time drove him crazy. Several times he'd thought of calling her but remembered their last conversation and put it back in his pocket without pushing a button. How could he explain to her that he hadn't meant what he said? He just wanted to have time with Kimberly. She was the daughter he never got to raise. This was his chance. Like the internet, he knew anything he said on the phone could be misconstrued. No, they needed to sit and talk face to face.

"Why don't you just go home?" J.C. leaned his guitar in its stand. Retrieving a pack of gum from his pocket, he offered a piece to Brendan. "I don't know a lot about women but do you see a gold band on this here?" He held up his left hand. "I don't think so. And do you know why?"

When J.C. didn't continue, Brendan knew his friend was waiting for him to ask. "No, why?"

"Because I know enough to not let one get under my skin. Problem with you is, that gal was already under yours before you got into the business."

"You're right, J.C. So what am I supposed to do?

I don't want to hurt her; I just want the chance to be a father to Kim. If I have to take legal action to do it, I will."

"Dang it." The barreled man slapped his leg in agitation. "Why don't you just do what you want? Marry the gal and get it over with."

"She won't marry me as long as I'm touring."

"So don't tour. It ain't no skin off my nose if you let your future son-in-law build you that theater he has in mind. That lot across from my place in Branson is still for sale."

"I don't know…" His voice trailed off as he began to pace the sound cubicle. He had little room but to turn and face his friend. "What if she won't have me?"

"Won't have you? Man, what do you think the woman is waiting for?"

Brendan laughed for the first time in days. "J.C. I don't know what I'd have done without you all these years."

"Don't get all gooey on me. Just get your tail in that jeep and back to that little gal and her kids where you belong."

Brendan had not hesitated taking J.C's suggestion. They had run through one more track then he'd tossed his go bag in the back of the Cherokee and headed north. He'd made a mandatory stop in Ada Oklahoma for much needed sleep. While people around the country enjoyed Thanksgiving dinner and football, he had driven all day. Now, he sat parked in front of the little cottage. A large teddy bear kept him company from the passenger seat. The bear had listened to his ramblings all the way from Austin.

J.C. had made a valid point, echoing Jennifer's sentiment of his career wasn't on the road. He was a performer. He could do that anywhere. The war within him raged with each passing mile. Would people come to Branson to see him? At this point in his career could he afford to drop off the touring circuit for more than a handful of dates a year?

On the other hand, he knew Stephanie would not stand for less than commitment from him. She didn't want, nor did she deserve a part-time figure in her life or that of Kim and Max. He knew she would settle for him being in the kids' life and not ask for anything from him for herself. She had never asked anything of him. Only when he hadn't offered the love she desperately wanted, had she given up and walked away. He didn't want her walking away again. Things were different. He was different. Now he had to prove to her... and to himself... where his priorities lay.

He reached for the door handle in time to see Stephanie switch off the porch light. She had given up on him again, at least for the night.

"Let's head to the hotel and get some sleep, Teddy." He ruffled the teddy bear's ears. "Tomorrow is going to be a long day and you have a new friend in your future."

CHAPTER 13

"Bedan!"

Max broke free of her hold and nearly tumbled off the bottom three steps in his haste to get to his friend. Brendan caught the toddler, swinging him high in the air. Her son's giggles bounced off the ceiling, sending them around the front hall in a stereo effect.

"Hey, buddy! Good to see you. You doing okay?"

"Yep. You missed my bifday. I'm this many." Her son used both hands to manipulate three fingers in an upright position.

"I know. I'm sorry. I was helping a friend, but you know what? I brought you a surprise. Can you wait here while I go get something?"

Max squirmed to get down and followed Brendan to the door. Stephanie smiled at the picture they made. If only things could work out.

Brendan went out the screen door then turned to

Max.

"You wait right here. Close your eyes so you don't see your surprise til it's time. Okay?"

Stephanie stepped up behind her son and gently covered his eyes. She felt his long lashes sweep her fingers as he closed them. He liked surprises and was not about to be caught peeking but the extra precaution wouldn't hurt. She watched as Brendan opened the passenger door of his Jeep and unbuckled the largest teddy bear she had ever seen with the exception of the one in the Chocolate Factory downtown. The stuffed monstrosity even looked big compared to the adult assisting the toy up to the house. With each stride, the bear appeared to be walking ahead of him. She could not contain her laughter.

"What's funny, mommy?"

"You'll see, sweetheart. He's almost here. Keep your eyes closed and I'll help you walk into the parlor. We'll wait there." She guided them back a few steps then turned him towards the room. They'd just cleared the doorway when she heard the screen shut behind Brendan and his companion.

"Is Max here? I want to meet my new friend?" Brendan's normal baritone went even deeper, taking on the voice of Teddy.

Stephanie removed her hands and her son yelled as he barreled across the room and into the duo. She quickly removed her phone from her pocket and snapped a picture. Max was doing his best to wrap his arms around the over-stuffed, milk chocolate colored bear with the big red bowtie as he smiled from ear to ear and pressed his cheek against the bear's tummy. Brendan continued to hold the bear while the two got acquainted.

"I told Teddy here that you had a birthday yesterday and he wanted to come home with me." Brendan sat the bear down in front of the sofa so he could remain propped up more at Max's height. "Do you like him?"

"I wuv him! He will be my bestest fend."

"I'm glad."

"Sweetie, why don't I put a movie in for you two while Brendan and I go to the kitchen? What do you think Teddy would like to watch?"

"Bob."

"Bob the Builder it is."

Stephanie started the DVD. When she turned, Brendan had already left the room. She clipped the gate in place then went to the kitchen where he was putting the kettle on the burner.

He looked so natural in her house, making himself at home. She skirted around the small prep island, putting distance between them as she went to the cupboard for mugs and sat them on the table. With the crispness in the late November air, she selected an Apple Cider for each of them. Though she avoided looking his direction, she was aware of him watching her as she opened the envelopes then deposited a tea bag in each cup.

"Excuse me." She barely acknowledged him as she stepped around him to the drawer for spoons. Now that they were alone, she remained cool. While she had missed him as much as her children, she was not about to let that show. Their last discussion left a lot to be hashed out before she would allow herself to envelop the happiness she felt at being near him again. If they were to have any form of a relationship, Brendan needed to understand he could not just come and go as he pleased and expect her to be waiting for his return. She had done that once.

He adjusted his position, allowing her just enough room to open the drawer. Only after she had returned to the table did he move completely, reaching for the cabinet doors above the stove.

"Spices up here?"

Before she could reply, he had opened the doors and reached for a quart mason jar with cinnamon sticks. He unscrewed the jar lid and took out two then closed the lid and put the container back in its place.

She continued to watch his movements as he carried the tea kettle over to where their cups sat and poured water over the tea bags before depositing a cinnamon stick with each one. The heat activated the pungent spice. Stephanie sat in one of the chairs and closed her eyes for a moment, inhaling the little extra touch he had added to the beverage. When she opened them, he was sitting across from her, stirring his drink with the spicy twizzle.

"We missed you yesterday."

"You did?"

She gave him a slight nod in reply.

"I'm sorry. I really didn't anticipate being gone as long as I was. J.C. and I finished up his recording as quick as we were able then I was on the road right after. I stopped in Ada for sleep and got in last night. You were turning the porch light out as I pulled up."

"You could have come in."

"I didn't want to disturb you or wake the kids. How was your Thanksgiving?"

The small talk was trying her nerves. They had a lot to discuss but they were both sidestepping the issue that could become a volatile conversation. She stuck her toe in, testing the topical waters.

"You were gone almost two weeks, Brendan. You never even bothered to check in." She surprised herself when her voice remained calm. "You can't do that when kids are involved. And you can't bring presents every time you return thinking that makes up for your absence."

He took a napkin from the holder, folded the paper in half and laid it next to his mug. After giving his cider a final stir, he placed the cinnamon stick on the napkin. Stephanie watched his precision movements, waiting for his response. Instead, he picked up the mug, gently blew across the surface then took a tentative sip. All without acknowledging she had said anything. He sat his drink down, still holding the handle. His silence made her want to scream at him, but little pitchers have big ears. Instead, she leaned across the table and spoke in a low, but firm tone.

"Brendan. Are you listening?"

When he finally looked at her his eyes held a sadness she had only seen one time before. The day they buried his brother.

"I hear you, Steph."

"And?"

"In my defense, the bear was a birthday present, not a peace offering to a three year old. Look, I'm sorry I insinuated we take this to court…"

"Insinuated?"

"Wait." He held up his hand to stop her. She clamped her lips together and waited. "Let me finish. I don't have any rights to Kimberly. I would never try to take her away from you. We are adults. We should be able to discuss this calmly and come to an agreement."

"What do you suggest?"

"Have dinner with me one night next week. We won't have to worry about interruptions or the kids overhearing anything that might upset them."

"Dinner?"

"That's all I'm asking. I haven't thought of much else but our last conversation for the past two weeks. I'll tell you what I've come up with, you share your opinion and we do it over a nice meal."

Part of her wanted to refuse. To tell him in no uncertain terms that any of his suggestions were futile and that once the wedding was over, she didn't want to see him again. But she knew that wasn't true. If nothing else, his time away had shown her how quickly he had become a part of their lives and opened up her heart to possibilities. Possibilities she had never deemed an option in their past.

Her heart was the other side of the coin. She still loved Brendan and wanted to believe theirs was a fairytale that could have a happy ending. But foremost she was a mother and she had to put her children first. Her mind kept going back to the same thing. Could they make their family work with Brendan touring? She knew other artists did but she'd also seen enough tabloid stories to know that temptation on the road was strong. She had heard the adage that where there was no trust, there was no love. Did she love him enough to trust him? Or would she always be wondering who he was with?

"You're back!"

Kimberly's arms encircled Brendan's neck and she planted a kiss on his cheek. Then stepped back, her face flushed with the realization of what she'd done.

"I'm sorry. I…"

"It's fine, Kim. I'm glad you wanted to do that. What have you been up to?"

"Final dress rehearsals for the Christmas play start this week. Will you be able to come?"

Stephanie saw the shadow cross her daughter's face. Kim had already acknowledged the fact Brendan might miss things like school plays yet she was hopeful, guarded but anticipating he might say yes. She looked at Brendan as he flashed a star-quality smile while wrapping an arm around Kim's waist, pulling her close.

"You just tell me when and where. I'm not going anywhere again until after the wedding. I'm still working out the rest. Okay?"

"Super." This time, she delivered a hug with full enthusiasm, nearly toppling him out of the chair. Their laughter filled the kitchen, attracting bellows of Mom from down the hall. Max might have a new buddy in Teddy, but he wanted to be with the rest of the party in the kitchen.

"Kim, will you go let your brother out of the parlor, please?"

"Okay. Oh, can Becky spend the night tomorrow night? Her mom wants to do some Christmas shopping."

"Goodness. Today is Black Friday. I guess the holiday season has arrived. Of course, she can stay over."

"Cool. Can we decorate the tree tonight now that Brendan's here?"

"Sure. We'll order take-out."

They had a tradition of decorating the tree on Thanksgiving. Yesterday, no one seemed in much of a holiday mood. The tree stood in the corner of the parlor pretty much matching their mood, dark and lonely. Now that Brendan was back, maybe they would all be in better spirits.

Kim came back to the kitchen, Max attempting to follow as he drug Teddy by an ear with both hands. The beast barely fit through the hallway. Finally exhausted in his attempt, Max stopped just outside the kitchen where he could see everything and snuggled against Teddy. He seemed content so Stephanie left him there. She took a drink and watched as Brendan and Kim entered their own conversation. Kim loved to decorate for any holiday but Christmas was her favorite. Her hands moved constantly as she talked a mile a minute. She told him about the small tree she put up in her room and that Max would get his own tree if he wanted but that he had to be five. Brendan cast a sideways glance her direction and winked as he followed his daughter's chatter.

His daughter. Stephanie realized that while she knew Brendan was the father, she had never referred to Kimberly in any way other than Matthew's daughter. The man listening to her now was filling a void Kim had carried for a long time. As she watched the two of them, she knew they deserved the opportunity to form a bond Stephanie had never anticipated.

"Mind if I hang around? I've not decorated a Christmas tree in years." He stood and took their cups to the sink, rinsed them then put them in the dishwasher as he spoke. He leaned against the counter, ankles and arms crossed waiting for her response. If he just wouldn't smile as if he knew the answer.

Stephanie hesitated. David carried the tree down from the attic every year but no man had helped them decorate a tree since Matthew. Putting up the Christmas tree on Thanksgiving was a family tradition he had brought to their home. His first tree since the death of his parents had been theirs as a couple. She knew the gesture had been difficult for him in the beginning but he said their marriage was a time for a fresh start for both of them. Was she starting over again?

"Come on, I'll show you where Mom stashes the decorations." Kim was already side-stepping her brother and his friend as she headed for the stairs that led to the attic above the second floor. "Dave set the tree up a couple of days ago so the branches could fluff out."

"Do you mind, Steph?"

"No, I don't mind. Be nice having a tall person

around." She recognized this as a great opportunity for Brendan to learn more about Kim's childhood.

Each year, she and Matthew had chosen a Hallmark ornament for the tree depicting a milestone in their daughter's life. The first ornament had been her sonogram picture in a pink frame, Cinderella's glass slipper the year she took her first steps and a white bunny riding a sled made from a box of Crayola crayons the year she started kindergarten. There were nine other ornaments for Kim as well as an ornament for each year the three of them had been together. She had continued the tradition on her own with Max. This year she might need to find a teddy bear similar to his new friend or drums… silent ones.

She helped Max move Teddy back to the parlor then called in a pizza order. She had just put a Christmas movie in when Brendan came down the stairs carrying two large tubs, one on top of the other. Stephanie hoped his stage training helped him find his footing as he descended the steps because there was no way he could see where he was going. Kim followed him with the lighter tub containing the tree lights.

"There's still several tubs left, Steph. We just brought the ones that said TREE on them."

"That's fine. We'll worry about the rest of the decorations Sunday after dinner."

Stephanie took the top tub from his load and put it on the sofa table. Brendan sat his next to the other one then turned towards the tree, rubbing his hands together with anticipation.

"Okay, coach, where do we start?"

"The lights always go on first." Kim sat her container beside the tree and removed the lid.

"We check to make sure they all work when we pack them away but there are usually some bulbs that need replacing."

After plugging in the power strip they used to turn all the strings on and off, she took the first coil and handed the spool to Brendan. Kim plugged the string in and when all the lights came on, she showed him how she meticulously wrapped each branch.

"Why don't you just wrap the string around the tree?" Brendan gradually unwound the lights from their spool while Kim worked her way in and out of each limb.

"If you go the length of the branch instead of around the outside the tree seems lit up all the way through." Stephanie hid her smile as she began unpacking the ornaments as her daughter continued. "Besides, it's a way cool effect when you lay underneath and look up through the lights. I'll show you when the tree is finished."

Three hours and two pizzas later, Brendan held Max up to place the angel on the top. Stephanie stepped to the doorframe and turned off the room lights. The tree seemed to pulse with a warmth she had not felt in the little Victorian cottage. For the first time, the house held the presence of being a home.

She brushed away the beginnings of tears as she watched Kim take Brendan's hand, drawing him down to the floor and showing him how to go head-first under the tree to look up through the branches, seeing the color-laden branches from a new perspective.

"Wow."

"Cool huh?"

"Absolutely cool."

Stephanie left the duo in conversation as she scooped up her dozing son and carried him upstairs. Tucking him into his new bed, she thought about how right everything seemed tonight. There were still lots of things to work out but she wanted this to be Brendan's home, too. She just wasn't sure how to get past his job and what they'd all gone through the past two weeks. Maybe he did have a solution, but other than him giving up touring she didn't see one.

When she returned to the parlor, Kim was gone.

"She got a text from Becky wanting to know if she could come over. I told her to go ahead and that I'd fill you in. I hope that's okay?"

"Yes. I swear we need a secret tunnel for those two girls to go between houses." She wasn't going to tell him Kim had texted her after she got to Becky's. Let him think he'd done the parent thing.

"They do seem pretty inseparable."

Stephanie started to gather up the ornament packaging when Brendan took her by the hand, encouraging her to join him under the tree. As she lay beside him, their fingers laced together, she was in awe of the view. She had started viewing the tree from this angle with Matthew and continued the experience with Kim after they'd moved down here. Max wasn't quite at the 'be still' this required. Now, here she was with her one true love. She exhaled slowly, balancing on the precipice of tranquility. She wasn't quite at peace yet.

"What's on your agenda for tomorrow?"

"I need to finalize some details for Jennifer's wedding and maybe some housekeeping in preparation for the rest of the decorations. Why?"

"Let me take the kids tomorrow. We could do some early Christmas shopping, maybe spend a little time at Silver Dollar City. Their Christmas Festival is going on so lots of things for them to see. Give you some time to yourself."

She felt the momentary calm leave her like a whispering soul and the stiffness she had experienced since Brendan's return to her life fill the void. She knew in her head the children were safe with him, self-assured he would give his life for them as if they both were his own. Kimberly would be over the moon at the prospect of spending the day with him. But what if something happened? Would he know what to do if Max got hurt somehow? Or separated from them? Silver Dollar City was a big place for a small boy to disappear. Her chest tightened as imagined panic rose within her. Then the quiet voice of reason floated amongst the twinkling lights.

"They will have a blast. Everything will be fine." With each word, he moved his thumb rhythmically across hers. "You have to learn to trust me, angel."

Trust. That was the one thing holding her back. She not only needed to trust him with the children, but with her heart as well. Was she ready to take the leap? She didn't think so. But baby steps? Maybe.

"What time do you want to pick them up?"

"Eight? I can take them to breakfast at Myrtie May's before we leave town."

"Max gets car sick on the curvy roads. How about ten? That will allow time for his breakfast to settle and his Dramamine to kick in."

He turned loose of her hand and scooted out from beneath the tree then stood and extended his hand to help her up. He pulled her close to him then wrapped his arms around her waist. They stood together in the glow of the colored lights, suspended in the moment of acceptance as Brendan dipped his head to brush her lips with his. Her heart skipped a beat as she braced her hands against his firm chest, letting the tenderness of his kiss penetrate her soul. She knew in that moment she had opened the door to something she had wanted so long ago.

He broke the kiss then looked at her and smiled.

"I'll see you in the morning."

She stood, with her fingers against her lips as if holding his kiss in place as she heard the front door click shut.

CHAPTER 14

Not knowing where Brendan had in mind for dinner, Stephanie had chosen her go-to business casual. She hadn't realized at the time she took the black dress pants and white silk blouse from her closet, that Brendan would choose the same outfit he'd worn the night of the gala. They looked like a real couple as they sat across from one another at Ermilio's. Brendan had shown up at the cottage and suggested they walk the few blocks back up the hill to the Italian Restaurant.

Ermilio's had earned several awards including Best Italian Restaurant in Arkansas. Considering Eureka Springs was a dot on the map compared to larger cities such as Little Rock, which spoke volumes for the owner and his team. He had worked with Stephanie a few times since she launched Planned to Perfection, catering small parties. The food and the service fit her idea of what an event should be. Perfect.

She was surprised they did not have the customary wait. Ermilio's was open from five to nine every evening, seven days a week except for January when they were closed for vacation. During the busier season, waiting up to ninety minutes was not uncommon. While they never accepted reservations, she decided Brendan may have had a little pull when they were barely in the door before being seated at one of the few tables for two in a quiet corner.

The black and white décor accented with tan drapes gave the place an elegant yet comfortable feel. Romantic music played softly throughout the entire restaurant. If he had plans to seduce her into submission, he was sadly mistaken. Yet she understood this was the perfect public place to have an adult conversation. Talking was becoming more natural between them when they had others in their company but this was different.

They had stayed on general topics during the customary Sunday dinner. Afterwards, the house had become a flurry of activity as they put the last of the Christmas decorations in place. Some held stories, which Kim shared. Stephanie noticed a touch of sadness return to her daughter as she talked about ones specific to Matthew, such as the wreath her Girl Scout troop made her the Christmas after he died. A green wreath with Blue and silver ball ornaments and an America's Finest Ornament from Military Republic hanging from the bow to swing in the center opening. Since their move down here, the wreath had taken a place of honor above the small table that held his academy photo and a velvet box with his badge.

"We didn't get to talk about your outing with the kids." Stephanie opened with what she thought would be the perfect segue to their pending discussion. "They had a great time, Saturday. Kim was still telling me every detail as she put her head on the pillow and fell asleep mid-sentence."

"If I hadn't thought you needed the time to yourself, I'd have asked you to come along.

"That and you wanted an outing with permission this time." She didn't attempt to hide the smile. While she had been furious and frightened at the time, she understood that everything happened for a reason though purpose might not be clear at the time. The secret outing had brought everything out into the open. Now, they needed to figure out the best way to move forward.

"That too. Seeing over six million Christmas lights through Max's eyes was an experience. I don't think his mouth closed from the moment we walked through the gate until he fell asleep on my shoulder on the way to the tram."

"I've never been. Maybe I'll take them next year." She hoped he didn't notice she was careful to eliminate him. Not that she didn't want him along, she just wasn't ready to make plans for something that might never happen. Who knew where Brendan would be in three months, six or ten.

"That would make a nice family tradition. I overheard several say they had come as kids with their parents and now were bringing their own."

The waitress brought a basket of fresh, hot bread along with butter and roasted garlic cloves. They agreed to share an appetizer of pesto bread rounds. Stephanie knew she would need to walk back and forth to the Crescent every day for a week to work off the meal but Ermilio's had won their awards for a reason. They both ordered iced tea as well as their entrees. When the waitress left, Brendan continued.

"Speaking of family tradition, you and Matthew created several. Your children are very lucky."

"Didn't you grow up with traditions? Your folks seem the type to go all out."

"I don't recall. A lot of my childhood memories were erased with the alcohol. Sad, isn't it?'

"I don't imagine being on the road allows you the opportunity to make your own."

"No. I didn't realize until this weekend with you and the kids how much I've missed out on. I'd like to change that, if you'll help me."

"I don't know, Brendan. I mean, I'd like to but…"

"But what? Stephanie, I don't know what you want from me."

"Don't you?"

"I told you that at some point you have to trust me, angel. I didn't mean just with the kids."

"I know. There was a time when I would have trusted you with my life."

"And now?"

Now? Could she go through the heartbreak again? She didn't know if she would have had the courage to walk out on him the first time if Matthew hadn't been there to catch her. Now, she was on her own. Frankly, she was tired of doing things alone.

While he'd had the kids Saturday she had taken

care of last minute tasks for Jennifer's wedding then rode the trolley downtown. Wandering by herself in shops selling more delicate items, places she wouldn't have dared take a three-year-old in, had been sheer heaven. She had felt like a real grown-up as she searched for the perfect wedding gift for Jennifer and David. Afterwards she stopped for tea and salad at Myrtie May's before returning home to the quiet cottage where she curled up on the sofa and watched holiday movies on the Hallmark Channel. Those shows always had the happy ever after ending she wanted for her life. Was that possible outside of a Hollywood script?

The waitress brought their salads. They had both chosen the Too Blue for You chunky blue cheese dressing. Stephanie ordered hers on the side, while Brendan's was generously drizzled across the top. A testament to their similarities as well as differences. Both attributes they'd need if things were to work out between them.

She took a couple of bites then laid her fork down and put her hands in her lap, choosing her words carefully when she spoke.

"My life isn't what I have to think about. The children are always foremost in my mind."

"I understand that. I can do that, too, if you'll give me a chance."

Stephanie placed her fork across her partially-eaten salad and moved the plate to the side before placing her elbows on the table and lacing her fingers together beneath her chin.

"I'm listening."

Brendan slid his plate next to hers then took a

long drink of tea. Was he stalling? Surely, he had rehearsed his pitch multiple times over the past few days. Or was he nervous about his proposition? She knew whatever he had in mind was new territory for him.

"After being included on your Sunday dinners, the field trips with the kids and helping to decorate for the holidays, I realized those were all things that I've been missing in my life. Not just the kids and not just you but the whole package. I want a family, angel. I want that with you and the kids."

"What about your career? I won't go over that discussion again. You know how I feel about your touring, yet I understand that's a part of who you are."

"No, it's what I do and I've been told by more than one person that there is a difference between what I do and where I do it." He leaned his forearms on the table in front of him. "Look, I can't just jump off the road and do something else. There is a whole slew of people who depend on me. Everyone from my manager and booking agent to the stage crew and my band. They all have families to provide for. I can't leave them in the lurch. All I'm asking is that you give me time to get things in order."

"How much time?"

"I don't know. I have a plan in the works. I can't say any more than that right now." He reached across the table and took both of her hands in his. "I have to go to Nashville right after the wedding for a meeting with my label. Hopefully, we can set up a timetable. Until then, angel, I just need you to trust me."

Stephanie saw the beseeching look in the brown pools that had won her heart that very first moment all those years ago. Now, as then, she could lose her soul if she weren't careful. She knew he had her heart. Her soul couldn't be far behind.

"I want us to work, Brendan. Last time it had been me asking for something. Now it's you. The difference is I'm willing to try."

"Me too, angel. Me too."

Their entrée's arrived and they spent the rest of the meal enjoying the food and talking about life in general while he ate his Filet Mignon she savored the Shrimp Provencale. She filled Brendan in on the latest wedding details and that she had scheduled his final tux fitting for later in the week. He asked questions about Kimberly's growing up, the things she knew he was now realizing how much he had missed in both her and Jennifer's formative years. Thankfully, both girls had fared well in spite of his absence.

As tempting as the Tiramisu sounded, they chose to skip dessert and walked back down the hill to the cottage. Kim and Max were both snuggled against Teddy watching Secret Life of Pets when they arrived, barely acknowledging the adults were back. Stephanie led the way to the kitchen where they fell into what had become an evening routine. Brendan discarded the kids' pizza remains while she put water on for tea. By the time the kettle whistled, Brendan had the cups waiting. They carried their drinks into the parlor and sat on the sofa to finish the movie with the kids.

The children were content, tree lights twinkled and she had as close to a promise of someone to share everything with as she could get for now. The peace she had been waiting for slowly wrapped around her like an ethereal warmth. She had his blessing.

* * *

Brendan knew the moment Stephanie accepted her potential future. The children, enthralled with the movie, were unaware of how their life would soon change. Maybe not much more than what they had experienced over the past few weeks, but on a more permanent level. He felt a glow of warmth envelope him and if he'd been a believer in ghosts, he'd stake his life on the fact that Matthew was okay with those changes.

He sat his cup on the side table then draped his arm around Stephanie's shoulders. He wasn't surprised when she snuggled in as she smiled up at him.

"Okay?"

He felt more than saw her nod as she closed her eyes and sighed. He took her cup and sat it next to his then laced their fingers together. For the first time he noticed the wedding band still in place, a sign she wasn't completely ready to let go but they were getting there. If she were willing to give him the time he needed, he would do the same.

The movie ended and Kim came over to them.

"Munchkin is asleep. I'm going up to bed. Goodnight Mom, goodnight Dad." With that, she leaned in and kissed them both on the cheek then went upstairs as if this were a routine she followed every night. And she had called him Dad.

"Want me to carry him upstairs for you?"

"Thanks... dad."

She giggled as he got up, pulling her along with him then gently scooped up the little boy and snuggled him against his shoulder.

Upstairs, he leaned against the door jam, watching as she managed to undress Max and tuck him in without so much as a sound of disturbance and using only the light from the hallway to see. Brendan wasn't sure he could manage that. Must be a motherly trait. But there were plenty of other things he could do for Matthew's son. Matthew had been there for Kimberly, now it was his turn to return the gesture.

When she'd finished, they walked back downstairs hand in hand. Before she could step off the final step, he turned and pulled her into his arms. From this point, they were almost the same height. He cupped her face in his hands and kissed her goodnight.

"I have a string of meetings in Branson so I probably won't be around much before the wedding. I'll be here for Sunday dinners, but beyond that I can't make promises until I know how things need to play out on the business end."

"Do what you need to do. We'll be here."

With those words, she leaned in for another kiss and Brendan knew he was making the right decision.

CHAPTER 15

"Mom, these shoes are too tight." Kimberly entered Stephanie's room, wincing with each step. "I can't wear them."

"They're the only ones you have that go with the dress." Stephanie slid her pumps on. With everything happening over the past few weeks, she had totally forgotten Kim needed shoes. She bent down and inserted her index finger between Kim's heel and the inside of the shoe.

"Ow! What am I going to do?"

"My cream flats are in the closet. They'll be a little loose but you can get through the afternoon. Take your time walking down the aisle and you should be fine."

A light snow had fallen the night before. Christmas Eve morning dawned clear, crisp and beautiful. Four inches of the powdery dust created the illusion of a Christmas card scene, providing the perfect backdrop for a winter wedding.

Max woke her up at first light with his own rendition of Jingle Bells. He had no sooner stopped singing than he began asking for Brendan. That part had become routine over the past month. This morning she'd been able to assure her son he would see him today. The past three Sunday dinners had been the extent of his visits since their date. He had warned her that would be the case but trying to explain his absence to Max had been a bit of a challenge. Steph had finally resorted to telling her son that Brendan was on a secret mission for Santa. She hoped she hadn't been lying.

If Brendan was able to work out whatever he was trying to do to ensure he was a more permanent part of their life, she knew Santa would be granting her wish and a Christmas miracle would be involved.

Hearing voices in the foyer below, she did a final check of her reflection, frowning at what she saw. Lack of sleep over the past weeks were beginning to show. The teal fabric of her dress closely matched the shadows beneath her eyes. Adding a last pat of powder, she turned out the light and went downstairs.

"Stephanie!" An older replica of Brendan greeted her in a hug as she stepped off the final stair.

"Pop!" She hugged Bill Keane with delight then turned to the petite woman beside him. "Betty, it's good to see you." She kissed Brendan's mom on the cheek. "I thought you'd be at the hotel with Jennifer."

"We were. There's too much activity going on over there for this old man. Brendan suggested we drop in on you."

"I hope it's okay." Betty Keane fussed with the buttons on her coat as if she were unsure whether to unbutton them or not. She and Stephanie had never been close. Pop and she had a special bond all those years ago when they hoped for a different outcome between her and his son.

"Of course! I'm glad you came. Let me take your coats." As she hung them up an uneasy feeling settled in the pit of her stomach.

They'd talked to Brendan? Well, of course they would have. Had he told them about Kimberly? Stephanie hadn't given a thought to telling his parents though she always thought Pop might have suspected at the time. She did know they would accept Kim as one of the family. That's the kind of people the Keane's were. They'd done the same with her all those years ago when she'd first become a part of Brendan's life. Betty Keane had been a mother when she needed one.

"Come in and sit down. We have time before we have to be at the church."

"Mom, Max won't let me... oh, excuse me. I didn't know we had company."

"It's okay, Kim. They just arrived." Before she could say anything further, Betty stepped forward and took hold of Kim's hands.

"Bill, can you believe how much she's grown? Why, she looks just like Jennifer did at thirteen."

"Yes, she does."

Stephanie saw the warm smile shared by the couple. They knew and everything was fine.

"Honey, do you remember Mr. and Mrs.

Keane?"

"Sort of." Her daughter looked questioningly at the couple then her eyes widened.

"You're Brendan's parents. That makes you…"

"Your grandparents, little one." Betty cupped the side of Kim's face with one hand.

"I've never had grandparents before."

"Yes, you have, Kim. You just didn't know us." Bill joined his wife and granddaughter. "We're glad everything is out in the open now."

"How long have you two known?" Stephanie wasn't surprised by their revelation.

"We first noticed the resemblance at Matthew's funeral." Betty took a few strands of Kimberley's hair between her fingers. Both of my granddaughters have a habit of twisting their hair around their fingers when they're nervous or upset. She has the Keane brown eyes, too."

"You never let on. Why not?"

Bill led them into the parlor. When she was seated between the couple, Bill took hold of one of her hands.

"We figured you had your reasons. You'd tell us when the time was right."

"The two of you have been so good to me over the years."

"You and Debbie did the best with the hand you'd been dealt. Bill and I are proud of the way you handled things."

Stephanie turned and hugged Betty. "Thank you. That means a lot." She caught sight of the clock over past the woman's shoulder. "Goodness, look at the time! We need to get to the church. Kim, the shoes you were looking for are in the box on my bed."

"Can we help with anything?"

"Pop, would you mind making sure the back door is locked? Betty, I'll send Max down with Kim if you'd give her a hand getting his coat on. I just need to make a quick call."

* * *

Thorncrown Chapel opened up the world to guests filing into the woodland church. Brendan paced the native stone path leading from the parking lot to the secluded sanctuary. In a few minutes he would be handing the care of his eldest daughter to someone else. The thought made him smile. Jennifer had proven a long time ago she could take care of herself. David would have his hands full.

"So do I." He wasn't sure how, but he intended to convince Stephanie to marry him. Over the past few weeks he and David had put their heads together over designs for a new theatre. He couldn't leave the road completely but with Branson as a more permanent venue he would have more control over the time he had with Kim and Max, as well as Stephanie if she would let him.

"How do I look, Dad?"

Lost in thought, he hadn't noticed Jennifer come down the path. His eyes misted at the woman standing in front of him.

Her chestnut hair had been styled atop her head with a long curl down either side of her face, just visible beneath the edge of the simple, yet elegant veil. She had chosen the perfect gown for a late December wedding. Heavy satin with sleeves just touching the elbows, meeting matching long gloves. She carried her bouquet in one hand. Two red roses representing her and David stood just above five white roses, one for each year they had been together. She lifted the hem of her dress with her other hand to display white boots that came just above her ankles, the white laces tagged with what looked like pom poms for snowballs. The white fur stole draped over her shoulders finished the snow princess bride effect.

"Absolutely beautiful, sweetheart." He kissed her cheek "Thorncrown in November? Really? You do know the Crescent has a great venue for weddings, right?" He hoped his teasing would alleviate some of the nerves she had to be feeling.

"They're calling for more snow that will add to the blessing this chapel has to offer."

"If you're sure, shall we?"

She slipped her hand in the crook of his arm as one of the ushers opened the wooden doors. One step at a time, they walked towards the front of the gathering. At the altar, David smiled and he felt Jennifer's death grip on his arm relax. She was going to be fine.

"Bedan! Mommy, Bedan!" Max's voice rang above the soft music from the sound system.

A wave of laughter rippled through the congregation. Everyone settled down as Brendan handed Jennifer over to the groom then took his place in the first pew next to his parents. Stephanie and the kids sat on the other side of them. Max wasted little time in crawling across the group to sit on his lap. Glancing quickly at Steph, Brendan saw her nod her approval.

As the minister opened the ceremony a light snow began to fall, giving the chapel the effect of being in a snow globe. The tiny sparklers fell through the sun's rays all around the exterior of the glass enclosure, capturing the attention of the gathering for a few moments as they watched in awe of nature's beauty. David and Jennifer couldn't have asked for a more perfect accompaniment to their union. Brendan glanced at Stephanie just as she turned to look at him. She smiled hesitantly as she swiped at a tear on her cheek with her fingertips. He hoped they were happy tears.

As the ceremony concluded, he attempted to hand the boy back to her.

"Go with Bedan, Mom. Pease?"

"He has to help Jennifer, sweetie. We'll see him at the hotel."

Brendan sensed protest from his little buddy. "He's fine, Stephanie. If you're okay, that is?"

"We'll keep an eye on him and Kimberly, honey." Bill gave her hand a squeeze.

"All right. I need to gather Jennifer's things and take them to the car. I'll meet you at the reception."

* * *

The Crystal Room overflowed with well-wishers. Waiters carrying large silver trays bearing flutes of champagne gracefully made their way through the crowd. The gift table replaced the pumpkins and cornstalks of Halloween. In one corner sat the wedding cake of Jennifer's dreams.

Four graduating tiers of elegance graced the center of the table. Smooth white icing covered each layer as a base for the Victorian-inspired ornate décor. The base was decorated in white flourishes and white chocolate snowflakes in varying sizes and barely a shade darker than the coating, seemed to be swirl around the cake's background. The swirling snowflakes appeared to blow up to the next tear, surrounding an ornate oval frame of white holly leaves. Inside the frame was an edible print of David and Jennifer's engagement picture taken in the Crescent garden. The next tear replicated the bottom but with smaller snowflakes as did the anniversary tier. The very top, Jennifer's bouquet had been duplicated in chocolate, right down to the trailing of holly leave and berries down the full length of the cake for a pop of color.

Jennifer had worked with the resident pastry chef to take the cake from her sketches to his talented fingers. She had been adamant that not a single bit of fondant be on the cake. She had also ordered one hundred chocolate cake pops, dipped in white chocolate then drizzled with red icing.

Somehow Stephanie had to keep an eye on Max or he would be going to bed with a tummy ache and she didn't want Kim to have to deal with that or call Marge in the middle of the night on Christmas Eve. When Jennifer said she wanted to get married on Christmas Eve, Stephanie had risen to the task on her busiest night of the year.

While the reception would continue without her, Stephanie had someplace to be. As inviting as the crowd of partiers filling the dance floor appeared, she would have to enjoy someone else's in the New Year. Checking her watch, she realized she would have just enough time to drop the kids off before she and Santa would begin their rounds.

"Mom, can we go for pizza with Granny and Pop?" Kimberly came running up to her in stocking feet, having given up the shoes as soon as they'd entered the ballroom. Brendan's parents were close on her heels with Max walking between them.

Stephanie smiled at the sight of her children with grandparents. She admired the Keanes. The couple seemed to still be deeply in love. Not just content but truly happy, as if they had never left their honeymoon. Regardless of what happened between her and Brendan, Stephanie knew these people would always be family.

"I guess so." Remember, straight to bed when you get home. Marge is just down the street if you need anything." She crouched down to Max's level. "You mind your sister if you want Santa to come tonight."

"Okay."

"We'll stay with the children, Stephanie. Don't worry about a thing."

"Are you sure, Betty?"

"Absolutely. I don't mean to invite ourselves but we'd like to be there when they wake up on Christmas morning."

Stephanie felt the tears pooling as she gave Betty a hug, whispering against her ear as she did so. "We are so blessed to have you in our lives, no matter what happens."

When she stepped back, she saw tears in the woman's eyes but a smile shone bright.

"That's settled then." Bill scooped Max up into his arms. "Ready for pizza, buddy?"

"Pizza!"

"Kim knows where the key is hidden. There's a guest room at the end of the hall on their floor. Make yourselves at home." She turned to Kim. "You two behave. I will try not to be too late."

"We'll be fine Mom. See you in the morning." Kimberly reached up to give her a quick kiss to the cheek then took hold of Betty's hand. "I know the best place for pizza but we'll have to order it from the lobby. We can't go in the Sky Bar."

Stephanie heard her daughter still giving instructions as they left the ballroom. After they had gone, she went in search of the bride and groom to let them know she was leaving.

* * *

"You make an appealing elf."

Coming from the bathroom off Jennifer's office, Stephanie froze. In the middle of the room stood St. Nicholas. Unlike her Santa's of the past, this one appeared a little taller and leaner. Rich brown eyes behind glassless spectacles danced with mischievous mirth.

"What are you doing here?" Her fingers shook as she attempted to pin her hair back.

"Why, it's Christmas Eve little lady." His voice

was a poor Santa imitation as he spoke matter-of-factly. "We have presents to deliver."

"A date in a restaurant full of people was one thing. But if you think I'm going riding through the woods alone with you in the dark, you're loony!"

"What are you afraid of, angel?" He dropped the beard from his chin and removed the spectacles. The man held the powers of a wizard in those eyes.

"Of being hurt; my children being hurt." Her voice wavered in her own ears. "I know you say you have a plan and I'm trying to give you the time you asked for but I don't think I'll ever get over you. I'm resolved to that, but I won't let our front door revolve around your comings and goings."

"What if I said you were right?"

"If I didn't know better, I'd say you've been drinking."

"There's nothing more sobering than realizing you've lost all that's important."

She couldn't allow the sweetest eyes she'd ever known seduce her. Not tonight, not ever. Like most every other woman in the world, she was addicted to chocolate and his brown eyes were of the richest temptation. Chocolate was her weakness… and so was Brendan Keane. A tap at the door broke the spell and she stepped back as the door opened.

"Hey you two." Jennifer stepped inside. "I'm melting in this gown. I need to change clothes. Stephanie can you give me a hand before you leave? I can't find a single bridal party member anywhere in that crowd."

"Sure."

"I'll wait for you downstairs. The sleigh is

loaded and ready."

Families, children were counting on her. She would not let them down and he knew it. Besides, at this late hour they would need the magic of Santa to make all of the stops and be home before daylight. She had no choice.

"Put your beard back in place, Santa. We have work to do. I'll be down in a few minutes."

Specks of glittering crystals captured by the moonlight danced across their path. There had been several years when they'd had to use the carriages. This year enough snow had fallen, blessing them with the ability to use the sled. A pair of buckskin mares pulled the heavy-laden vehicle with ease over the snowy roads and more continued to fall.

Christmas carols replaced their previous serious conversation. As they drove through the winter wonderland, Stephanie knew even if things didn't work out, she would never forget this holiday in all its ups and downs. This Christmas season held a new sparkle because of Brendan's presence.

She snuggled deeper into the heavy quilts and fur robe that kept them warm. With the full moon and two large coach lanterns to guide them through the night, she directed Santa in the turns and stops.

Each house brought her face to face with a reality. Nothing in her life compared to what these people experienced every day. Despite the lack of necessities, each family gave something in return. Some gave cherished personal items. Others shyly handed gifts they had made. Regardless of the origin, she knew each one came with the true spirit of the season. Love.

AN OZARKS CHRISTMAS

At every stop, Brendan got out first then grasped her around the waist and helped her down. Each time she found herself within kissing distance and each time, the spell was broken as the residents would open their door, calling them to come in.

At the last stop, Brendan helped her into the sleigh. After tucking the quilts tightly around her, he climbed in from the other side then pulled her close as he snapped the reins, setting the horses into motion. With the last of the presents delivered, she could go home to her own family.

"Brendan?"

"Hmm?"

"You said earlier about losing the important things in your life. What did you mean?"

"I'm leaving the road, Stephanie. You and the children are more important to me. I can't give you all the details just yet, but please, trust me when I say everything is going to work out."

A ray of hope tickled her senses. "I thought you said you had to tour?"

"I've spent the last thirteen years with a big hole, right here." He pointed to where his heart lay beneath the padding. "One look at you that night on the balcony and I felt the hole shrink. Finding out Kimberly is my daughter put the last stitch in place."

"What will you do? You said touring was your life."

"A wise woman pointed out that my life is performing. Touring is a vehicle so I need a new mode of transportation."

"What does that mean? That you're not going to

209

tour?"

"Has the cold numbed your brain, woman? I'm not going anywhere." Kissing her on the tip of her nose then continued. "So what can Santa bring you for Christmas?"

"I would like peace on earth, good will towards men."

"Anything else?"

"Oh… maybe a tiny box about like this." She demonstrated the size with her fingers. "The box would fit nicely in my stocking."

"Would it now?" He chuckled in amusement and pulled into a copse of trees on the outskirts of town and stopped the team.

"I have an early Christmas gift for you. After the Silver Dollar City project is complete, David is going to design and oversee the construction of my new theater."

"That's wonderful." Her squeal pierced the crisp air as she flung her arms around his neck. Her delight was momentary. He felt her still, then draw back.

"Where does that put us? I have to know, Brendan. I never stopped loving you and I never will."

Cupper her face in his hands, he drew her to him. Maybe I didn't do all the things I should have, angel. I was never there for you." He used his mitten-covered thumb to brush the tears from her cheeks. "I know you wanted to hear 'I love you'."

Laying a finger to her lips, he silenced her. "Despite all of that sweetheart, you were always on my mind. I love you and I don't want to be without you."

When he gathered her in his arms, her lips trembled as they found his. As snowflakes whispered through the branches above them Brendan felt a completeness he knew she had wanted from him so long ago and knew she felt the same.

* * *

"Bedan!"

Brendan's dad carried the boy downstairs and put him down at the bottom step.

Max propelled himself into his buddy's waiting arms. Sitting on the rug in front of the fire place he felt a warmth that had nothing to do with the burning logs. Arriving home just before dawn, he and Stephanie sat talking, until they'd fallen asleep against one another on the sofa.

"Merry Christmas, buddy." He settled the child into the crook of his arm. "Where's your sister?"

"I'm here, Dad. You're here early." Kimberly came into the room wearing the white pajamas with the Santa and sleigh pattern Stephanie had put on her bed before they had left for the church. Another tradition was that each of them received new pajamas to wear to bed on Christmas Eve. Max's were the same pattern but in red.

"I wasn't going to miss our first Christmas together. Besides, I have a gift for your mom that couldn't wait."

"For me?" Her look of surprise made him smile.

"Kim, get her stocking, please?"

Taking the stocking from her daughter, she eyed him quizzically.

"Dump it out, angel."

Among the candy and gaily-wrapped trinkets scattered on the floor lay a small, blue velvet box. He watched anxiously, her fingers trembling as she picked up the box she had described to him last night. She had not known at the time his dad was adding the gift to her stocking.

Brendan slid Max off his lap then took the box from her as he raised onto one knee. Lifting the lid, he held the open box in front of her. The diamond within danced in the firelight.

"Stephanie, will you do me the honor?"

He watched the tears spill down her cheeks as in a choked whisper, she uttered the dearest words he would ever hear.

"I will."

EPILOGUE

One Year Later

"What are you thinking about, Mrs. Keane?"

Brendan's voice came as a soft whisper from behind her as he stroked a path down the back of her black velvet dress before encircling her waist. Snuggling against him, she rested her head on his shoulder, gazing at the twinkling tree lights.

"How much has happened in the past year. Everything moved so quickly."

"I know." He nibbled on her ear and a giggle bubbled within her. He made her feel so young. She and Brendan had married on Valentine's Day. She had given him a heart-shaped box of chocolates. Inside, on top of the confections, she had placed a note, informing him he was going to be a dad again.

"When I stepped out onto the patio of the Crescent Hotel at the gala that night, I never imagined that I would be married, have three children including our son and I'm about to become a grandfather."

"A very handsome one, I might add." Reaching up, she stroked his cheek. Accepting the invitation he bent to nuzzle her neck. She felt her knees weaken. Succumbing to the passion that engulfed her, she turned to slide her arms around his neck. Standing on tip toe, she kissed him.

"Geeze, you guys."

They smiled at Kimberly's mock irritation. "Keep that up and Devlin won't be the baby any longer."

"What do you think, angel? Shall we add to the family?"

"I don't think so. Play all you want buster but I'm not going through labor ever again."

"You guys are gross. I'm going to take Becky's Christmas present to her. I won't be long." Kim was already reaching for her coat on the hook by the door.

"Not tonight."

"Mom, why not?"

Stephanie smiled knowingly as the bell over the front door jingled.

"Granny! Pop!"

"Hey there, kiddo." Bill grabbed her in a bear hug.

"Pop Pop." Max ran across the room, propelling himself at the older man.

"Hi there, tiger."

"Where's the baby, Steph? Is he sleeping?" Betty draped her coat on a hook as she spoke.

"No, Mom, Devlin's there in the cradle by the

tree watching the lights." She hugged her mother-in-law. Had it really been a year since they'd stood in this very room introducing the kids to their grandparents?

"My heavens, what a big boy." Betty picked up the cooing infant and snuggled him to her shoulder.

The cradle was the most precious baby gift they had received. Whiskers delivered his most recent piece of handiwork the day they brought Devlin home from the hospital. Through tears of love, she had watched as the old man gently took the newborn child from Brendan's arms and laid him in the cradle. The man stopped by often to see them. Brendan had even convinced him to join them for Thanksgiving dinner.

"Glad to know I'm loved." Brenda moved to slip an arm around his mother's shoulders, kissing her forehead.

"I believe my loving you is how we got this little guy." Stephanie joined them as they looked at their three-month-old son.

"So it is, angel."

The bell jingled again, followed by a chorus of Happy Holidays from the foyer as David and Jennifer came in.

"Hi Pop, Gran. When did you get in?" Jennifer moved slowly into the room with the obvious cumbersome weight.

"Late last night. We checked in to the hotel but didn't want to disturb you. You need all the sleep you can get while you can."

Stephanie took Devlin and placed him back in the cradle. Her eyes brimmed with unshed tears as she watched Brendan's mother cross the room to Jennifer and gently placed a hand on the protruding belly holding her first great grandchild.

"And my first grandchild." The thought had passed through Stephanie's mind multiple times over the past few months. She still had trouble relating to that one.

"Just a bit ago, dear." Betty placed her hand against Jennifer's tummy. Her smile broadened as little one gave a kick.

She moved to stand next to Brendan. As he talked with his dad and David, she silently slipped her hand in his. He winked, squeezing her fingers lightly.

"That boy of yours is really growing." Bill motioned towards Devlin.

"They all are, Dad. Max got a bike with training wheels for his birthday. Kimberly will be able to letter in track next spring just chasing him up and down the street. He wants to go everywhere, fast."

"He's a lot like you already." Raising their entwined fingers, Stephanie brushed a tender kiss across them.

"Speaking of my oldest son, can we give him and Kimberly one of their presents now?"

"Brendan, Christmas is tomorrow."

"I know, honey, but this is special."

"Presents? Where are they? Kimberly began peeking in her still-empty stocking and under the tree.

"You just can't wait any more than they can."

"Sue me. I love Christmas. So can we?" His tone cajoled her into submission.

"Oh, all right. Everyone over by the tree." Stephanie went to her desk. Opening the bottom drawer, she withdrew two gifts.

"Don't open this just yet." She handed a box wrapped in glittering purple paper with a gold tinsel bow to Kim. She handed one simply wrapped in striped paper of red and white to Brendan.

"Now?"

Now." Stephanie nodded. Perching on the edge of the sofa, she watched her daughter's face.

Tearing at the paper, Kimberly lifted the lid then removed the folded piece of paper from the box, her face held a puzzled expression. You could have heard a snowflake fall in the stillness. The anticipation was almost more than Stephanie could bear.

"Read it."

Mom, Dad. This says my name isn't Douglas anymore." Astonishment covered her face as she looked at Brendan. "Is this true? Am I really Kimberly Ann Keane?"

"Well, that depends on you." Stephanie handed him a pen. "We'd talked about it but you never said how you'd feel. Matthew Douglas was your father. He raised you long before I came into the picture."

"Dad, I think he'd understand. I mean, I still love him and miss him but from the moment you and mom made me, I was a Keane."

"Then you'll need this." He handed her the pen and pointed to the 'X' on the paper.

Kimberly out-shown the tree lights as she signed her name.

"Is that it? Is it official?"

"Close enough for me." Brendan kissed the tip of her nose. "That isn't the official document. We'll need to do that with a notary but I wanted to make sure we were on the same page before we took that step. You can put this copy in your scrapbook."

"Is that Max's present?"

"Yep. Effective January fifteenth, both of you are officially adopted."

"Can I please go to Becky's? We need to exchange gifts and I just have to tell her the latest."

"Let her go, Mom." Brendan grinned, elbowing her.

Stephanie threw up her hands in resignation. "Go. But be back in an hour. Your Dad and I have to leave in a few minutes. I'd like you to help your grandparents with Max."

"Okay."

"Is everything in the car?" Brendan pulled himself to a standing position.

"Yes. Alan called a few minutes ago. The carriage is loaded and ready. All we need to do is get dressed at the hotel."

"Good. Think we can find that copse of trees again this year?" His devilish grin flashed with mischief.

"Let's take an extra quilt just in case."

"I'll grab one and meet you in the jeep."

Stephanie watched as the love of her life took the stairs two at a time before turning her attention to the rest of the room. Pop and Max had moved to sit on the floor where they played with a truck the four-year-old received for his birthday. Betty, Jennifer and Dave sat on the sofa facing the fireplace, chatting. She looked in the cradle to see her newest son sound asleep. What a difference a year made. Everything seemed so right. This was the most perfect Christmas Eve Stephanie remembered ever having and it was all because of Brendan. She had the family she had always wanted with the man she had always loved.

THE END

ABOUT THE AUTHOR

Angela Drake

Angela Drake believes in happy endings, the magic of 'what if' and second chances. When not living vicariously through her characters, Angela spends her day working social media accounts for musicians and authors.

She enjoys time with her granddaughters, gardening, journaling, and a myriad of artistic pursuits. She shares a home in the Ozarks with her husband, two dogs and three cats. She loves networking with readers and writers through her Facebook, twitter Instagram and blog.